THE NEXT TO DIE

When a body is found under a pile of gravel at the foot of a bank, it looks as if the storm the previous night blew a cart-load over just as the man was passing underneath. But amateur criminologist Trevor Lowe notices that the soles of the dead man's shoes are caked with cigarette ash: clearly he never walked to the gravel site, but was carried there. It is the first of a whole series of murders. Can Lowe unmask the criminal — or will he be the next to die?

GERALD VERNER

THE NEXT TO DIE

Complete and Unabridged

LINFORD
Leicester

First published in Great Britain

First Linford Edition
published 2017

A catalogue record for this book is available
from the British Library.

ISBN 978–1–4448–3313–3

Published by
F. A. Thorpe (Publishing)
Anstey, Leicestershire

Set by Words & Graphics Ltd.
Anstey, Leicestershire
Printed and bound in Great Britain by
T. J. International Ltd., Padstow, Cornwall

This book is printed on acid-free paper

1

The Inn on the Moor

Such a storm as that which had raged for the past two days over Dartmoor had had no parallel for years. The drenching rain and sleet fell without cessation, lashed to fury by the gale that howled and whistled across the wide expanse of country, shrieking with demoniacal laughter round the high tors and roaring tempestuously over the valley.

It embraced the twisted chimneys of Ridgeway Manor and tore with clawing fingers at the age-old ivy that enwrapped the red-brick walls, and went racing on along Blackbarrow Coombe, tossing aside in its path the spoils of victory, and came out upon the exposed moorland with undiminished fury.

It left behind in its wake a trail of waste and destruction — telegraph wires slack and humming, fences broken down, and in every second field or meadow a fallen tree: mute evidence of its pitiless blast.

It tore at the coat of the tall man who, on this grey and tempestuous afternoon, was fighting his way unsteadily along the twisting main road that led upwards from the little village of Stoneford to the open moor. On every side, as he pursued his staggering course along the long gully of Blackbarrow Coombe, the ruthless work of the south-wester revealed itself. Near the end of the coombe he passed the tragic ruins of a belt of pine trees, laid low as if by one sweep of a mighty scythe, the red shields of their upturned roots a melancholy monument to the proud magnificence of the past. A little further along, the wooden shelter of a moorland shepherd had been carried bodily a furlong across some rough pasture-land and wedged between two beeches fifteen feet above the ground. The road itself was densely strewn with branches, large and small, torn savagely from the groaning trees, whose boughs swayed and tossed wildly as if in torment.

Several of these flying missiles narrowly missed the bent head of the man as he struggled doggedly forward, and he muttered a curse at every fresh escape.

The air was filled with a whooping, screaming, ceaseless clamour that imparted a sensation of breathlessness; and over all, that implacable note of the wind that was still rising in a steady cadence. The night that was coming would, if anything, it seemed, be worse than the day that was ending.

The tall figure, scarcely visible in the fading light, pushed resolutely on, apparently heedless of the chaos that whirled and screamed around him, his hands thrust deep into the pockets of his heavy overcoat, his tweed cap pulled down firmly over his eyes. Presently the narrow road came out into the open, with a wide expanse of upland on either side that extended in undulating country to the horizon and the colourless desolation of a leaden sky swept bare.

For nearly a mile he traversed this twisting track across the moor, fighting every inch of the way in the teeth of the gale, his cap a sodden rag, his coat in little better condition. At last the scenery to his right took on a sudden change. A long hillside rose at a gentle slope, and the road, skirting the foot of this, ended in a sort of bay, thickly wooded with tall pines, in the midst of which stood a low, ramshackle building.

The solitary walker stopped when he found himself in the shelter and comparative silence of this little oasis, and drew the back of a frozen hand across his streaming eyes. With his vision a trifle clearer, he looked at the almost illegible sign that swung from a post on the edge of the road, and made out in faded lettering the words 'Black Moor Inn'.

The exterior was not inviting. An English roadside inn, however small and however disappointing inside, usually contrives to show a face sufficiently attractive beyond its surroundings to entice at least the eye of a possible customer. But this one might easily have been passed unseen, so completely had its crude ugliness of design and the dingy tones of its bricks and tiles subdued themselves in long years of neglect to the neutral colouring of its background.

The clump of pines behind and at either side thrust out shadowy branches that overshadowed it, hiding it from the chance wayfarer until he had almost passed the low, narrow door. Two-storied and of considerable frontage, with a medley of decayed outbuildings huddled together beneath the trees at the rear, it looked what it had been for a century and a half — a mere place of call for wagoners, farm-labourers, shepherds, and the like, too far from better cheer.

The road branched in a fork in front of it and straggled away across the moor, losing itself in the approaching darkness of the night. Not a living soul moved within sight, not a solitary sheep even, as the man who had come to this desolate and inhospitable-looking place approached the door.

In response to his thrice-repeated jangling of a decrepit bell in the dark entrance passage, the door was opened and a rough-looking man appeared on the threshold. If it was some time since he had washed and shaved and changed the shirt whose sleeves were rolled up on two grimy, muscular arms, he had at least been sampling his own beer recently, and with appreciation, for he was both odorous and befuddled.

He eyed the visitor short-sightedly from small, bloodshot, red-rimmed eyes. 'Wot yer want?' he growled ungraciously.

'You got my letter?' said the man in the cap harshly.

The other started. 'Then you're — ' he began, and was interrupted.

'I am the man who wrote that letter,' snapped the stranger. 'No names, please, Box. Who else did you expect would want to come to the Black Moor Inn on a foul night like this?'

'I don't know,' mumbled Box, who was evidently the proprietor. 'But I wasn't sure it was you. I ain't seen yer fer years, 'ave I?'

'No,' retorted the man who objected to names. 'And when this business is over I don't suppose you'll ever see me again.'

Box muttered something thickly and opened the door wider. The stranger entered, and was shown into a bare, dusty apartment facing the tap-room across the passage, and furnished with three dilapidated cane-bottomed chairs, a rickety, beer-stained table, a disreputable horsehair sofa, and two flyblown hunting prints of the early forties. A small fire burned reluctantly in the rusty grate, from which every now and again a billow of acrid smoke belched out, adding unpleasantly to the already musty smell of the room.

The visitor looked about him disgustedly. 'Couldn't have chosen a better place than this if I'd had it specially built,' he said. 'I shouldn't think anyone comes here once in a blue moon, do they?'

Box shook his matted head. 'Not orfen,' he answered, his voice slurred with the amount of beer he had consumed. 'Get a shepherd or wagoner in now and again. Even then they never come in 'ere — no further than the bar.'

'How do you live?' asked the visitor, taking off his dripping cap and overcoat and flinging them on the sofa.

'Got a bit put by,' answered Box. 'Not a lot, but a bit.'

The other drew forward a chair, and, sitting down, spread his numbed hands to the meagre blaze. 'Pickings from the old days, eh?' He laughed; an unpleasant, jarring, mirthless sound. 'Well, this evening's job will put a cool hundred in your pocket.'

'So yer said in yer letter,' grunted Box.

'You didn't mention, though, what I'd got to do for it.'

The visitor twisted his head round and looked at the uncouth figure lounging in the doorway. 'You've got to do nothing,' he replied, 'except keep your eyes closed and your mouth shut.'

'That seems easy.' Box grinned slowly. 'Wot's the gime?'

'There is also another condition attached to the earning of that hundred pounds,' was the reply. 'The third condition is, mind your own business.'

'You ain't changed in all these years, 'ave yer?' grumbled the proprietor of the Black Moor Inn. 'Still as close as ever!'

'I find that it pays,' retorted the visitor, stretching out his feet to the fender and watching the steam rise from the soles of his boots. 'It is only fools who chatter.'

'Nobody could call you a fool,' said Box with grudging admiration. 'You were always a wise one, 'cept that once when — '

'Reminiscences are also dangerous,' snapped the other quickly, and Box muttered an apology. 'There's one thing, however, I will tell you,' the stranger went on immediately, 'because I've got to tell you. Do you know Elmer N. Jensen?'

Box drew in a sharp breath and his great gnarled hand closed until the knuckles gleamed white against the dirty skin. 'Do I know 'im!' he snarled, and his sallow face flushed redly. 'Yes, I know him — the 'ound. He lives in Ridgeway Manor — bought it from Sir Gordon Leyton a year ago.'

'So you know him, eh?' The visitor nodded approvingly. 'And there doesn't appear to be much love lost between you, either.'

'Love!' The innkeeper's thick lips curled back, revealing a row of yellow, broken teeth. 'I hate 'im!'

'That is even better than I hoped.' The man by the fire chuckled softly. 'Why do you hate Jensen?'

'Ain't I got cause to?' said Box, his red-rimmed eyes sparkling savagely. ''E 'orsewhipped me in the 'igh street down at Stoneford two months ago.'

'Oh, did he? What for?' asked the other curiously.

''Cos I spoke to Tim Wyler's daughter,' muttered the innkeeper. 'That's all.'

'That's not quite accurate, is it?' The stranger swung round and regarded him steadily. 'You must have done something else besides just speak to the woman.'

'Well ...' Box shrugged his massive shoulders. 'As a matter o' fact, I did try and kiss 'er — but it weren't none of 'is business, and anyway I was a bit merry, like.'

'You seem to be developing a habit of being a bit merry-like,' remarked the visitor, eyeing the landlord's blotched face and filmy eyes. 'You're getting too fond of your own beer, Box, much too fond.'

'What else is there to do in this forsaken 'ole?' was the sullen answer. 'An' anyway, I can do as I like, I s'pose.'

'Certainly, so far as I'm concerned,' answered the stranger. 'But you're a fool, all the same. You were a pretty smart fellow in the old days —'

'Thought you said reminiscences was dangerous,' interrupted Box sourly. 'And anyway, you didn't come 'ere ter give me good advice. Why did yer want ter know if I knew Jensen?'

The man by the fire took out a cigarette case, helped himself from its contents, and

10

lighted a cigarette. 'Because,' he answered slowly, blowing out a cloud of smoke, 'Jensen is coming here — tonight.'

Box uttered an exclamation. 'Comin' 'ere?' he cried hoarsely. 'What's 'e comin' 'ere for?'

'He is coming here to meet me, my friend,' replied the visitor, and his voice was as hard and brittle as glass. 'And after we have had a little talk, Elmer N. Jensen will go out into the storm again, but not as he came.' He shook his head. 'Most certainly not as he came.'

The innkeeper caught at the sinister inflexion in the tone of the last words, and advanced a step nearer to the figure by the fire. 'Wot yer mean?' he muttered. 'You ain't goin' ter — ' He broke off, the end of the sentence dying on his lips, and stared at the other in horrified silence.

'I am going to do just that,' came the answer, and there was no mistaking what 'just that' meant.

'You mean … *murder*,' whispered Box huskily, and the man by the fire inclined his head. 'But yer can't — not 'ere, any'ow,' said the landlord. 'I won't stand for that.'

11

'You'll stand for anything I like,' snapped his visitor harshly, 'unless you'd like a little note dropped to the local inspector of police.' He smiled as Box suddenly cringed back. 'I thought that would make you see things in a different light,' he added.

'But if anything happens to Jensen here, they'll blame me fer it,' cried the innkeeper fearfully. 'They know I've 'ad a row with 'im. I said at the time if I 'ad 'alf a chance, I'd do 'im in.'

'You needn't worry so far as your skin is concerned,' said the stranger. 'I've planned the whole thing carefully. There will be nothing here to incriminate you. Jensen will die, but he will not die here.'

Box drew the back of his huge hand across his wet forehead. 'Well, for 'eaven's sake don't get me into any trouble,' he whined. 'I don't care a tinker's cuss what 'appens to Jensen, so long as I don't get dragged into it.'

The stranger gave him a contemptuous glance. 'You always were a coward, Box,' he said. 'When the time comes, I shall want your assistance, but you needn't worry that it will involve you in any way if you keep your mouth shut. Now go and fetch me a drink — some decent whisky, if you've got any.'

The landlord hesitated, opened his mouth as though about to say something more, and then shambled off to the tap-room to attend to his unwelcome guest's needs.

The stranger stirred the fire to a blaze with his foot and drew his chair closer to the flames. Outside, the note of the wind had risen to a shriller key, and bursts of rain splashed and rattled on the window-pane.

Just the right kind of weather for his plans, reflected the visitor, as he sipped the neat whisky that Box had brought and waited for the arrival of the man who was at that moment forcing his way through the storm and walking all unknowingly to his doom.

2

The First to Die

Mr. Trevor Lowe, the successful dramatist, turned round from surveying the little village street through the coffee-room window of the Rose and Crown as his secretary entered.

'You're late,' he remarked. 'Breakfast has been ready this twenty minutes. I expect the bacon's ruined.'

'Sorry,' apologized Arnold White, coming over and warming his hands at the cheerful fire, 'but I didn't sleep very well. The storm kept me awake until just before dawn.'

'It was pretty rough,' admitted the dramatist. He went to the door and called for their breakfast to be brought. 'The weather's changed this morning, though, thank God,' he went on, returning and taking his seat at the table. 'Still a little blustery, but fine. I think we shall be able to continue our journey this morning to town.'

He and White had come down to

Devonshire to spend the weekend with some friends whom Lowe had not been able to find time to see for some months. They had been on their way back to London when the storm broke, and since it was impossible to continue the journey, had decided to put up at the Rose and Crown in Stoneford until the violence of the storm had blown itself out.

In spite of the whining of the wind and the patter of the rain outside, it was very comfortable within, and Trevor Lowe had found the peace of the old inn very restful. The two days that he had been forced to spend under its hospitable roof had provided him with a much-needed holiday, which under any other circumstances he would not have taken.

'I shall be sorry to leave this place,' said White as he attacked the plate of bacon and eggs that the rosy-faced country servant set before him. 'I should have liked to explore a bit now that the weather's cleared up.'

'So should I,' answered Lowe, pouring out two cups of fragrant coffee and pushing one across to his secretary. 'But we can't afford the time. We ought to get back at the latest today.'

Arnold White nodded, his mouth was too full for speech.

'Anyway,' the dramatist continued, 'you can have an hour to look about you. Now we're here, I want to run over and see Major Strickland at Coombe Vale. He's the chief constable for the district and used to be at school with me. It's nearly three years since I've seen him, and it's only about eleven miles from here. I'll take the car, and if you like to have a prowl round while I'm gone I can pick you up again here.'

White agreed eagerly. His enforced sojourn indoors had resulted in a longing to stretch his legs, and the prospect of a brisk walk over the windswept moor was very alluring. They had finished their breakfast, and the dramatist was standing by the window smoking a cigarette preparatory to setting out on his visit, when the need for that visit was rendered unnecessary.

A long-bonneted black car pulled up outside the inn with a jerk and a screaming of brakes, and a rather stout, red-faced man sprang out with surprising agility, considering his bulk, and entered the porch.

Lowe only caught the briefest glimpse of him, but it was sufficient. 'Strickland, by Jove!' he exclaimed; and without stopping to explain himself to the wondering secretary, hurried out of the coffee-room and made his way to the bar.

The red-faced man was in the act of raising a glass to his lips when the dramatist entered, and he paused with it halfway as he caught sight of him, his rather bulging blue eyes wide with astonishment.

'Lowe, by all that's wonderful,' he cried; and setting down his untasted brandy, grabbed his friend's hand and shook it vigorously. 'What in thunder are you doing in this neighbourhood?'

Trevor Lowe explained briefly.

'Well, I'm damned glad to see you,' said Major Strickland heartily. 'What about coming over to dinner with me this evening?'

'Can't, old man,' said the dramatist, shaking his head. 'I'm going back to London almost directly.'

The chief constable's brick-red face fell. 'Oh, that's hard luck,' he said, gulping down his drink. 'I've got to go up to Blackbarrow Coombe now. Only called in here for a second on the way to get a warmer.' He brightened up as a thought struck him. 'Look here — why not come along with me, and then we can come back here and have lunch together before you start for town? That won't delay you very long.'

'It's an idea, certainly,' said Lowe with a smile. 'Where are you going?'

Major Strickland frowned. 'Local inspector phoned me at eight o'clock this morning,' he replied. 'Elmer N. Jensen — he's an American chap who lives at Ridgeway in the valley — has met with an accident.'

'An accident?' Lowe raised his eyebrows.

'Well, Rooper — that's the inspector — is not quite sure whether it's an accident or what it is,' said Major Strickland. 'That's why he phoned for me. And, by Jove, I'll have to be going,' he added hurriedly. 'Are you coming?'

Lowe nodded. 'Can I bring my secretary?' he asked.

'Yes, of course,' said Strickland. 'Will you have a drink before we go?'

'No, thanks,' said the dramatist. 'Only just had breakfast.'

'All right then, meet me at the car,' cried

the chief constable, and bustled out.

Lowe called White, hurriedly explained where they were going, and struggled into his overcoat. A few seconds later they were seated in Strickland's powerful Buick, rushing through the keen, frosty air towards the beginning of what was to prove one of the most startling series of crimes that had ever appeared on the front pages of a daily newspaper.

The havoc of the storm was visible on all sides as they drove along the gully of Blackbarrow Coombe, and twice the car had to slow down and scrape by a fallen tree that partially blocked the road.

They had proceeded for about three miles when the track sloped sharply upwards. The bank on one side of the road gave place to open moorland, while the other rose steeply, almost like a cliff, and ran parallel with the road for some considerable distance. Presently further along there appeared signs of building operations in progress on the top of the cliff-like bank. Several heaps of bricks became visible, mountainous piles of slates, and then the half-completed skeleton of a low, one-storied building.

As the car rounded a slight bend in the road, they came suddenly, a few yards ahead, upon a group of men. Amongst them was a uniformed constable, and they all appeared to be looking down at something that lay on the ground by the side of a heap of gravel.

'Here we are,' grunted Major Strickland as he brought the car to a standstill. Getting down, he approached a tall, thin, lanky figure that had detached itself from the group and started towards the car. 'What's happened, Rooper?'

The grizzled inspector saluted. 'Rather serious business, I'm afraid,' he said in a doleful, melancholy voice. 'It's Mr. Jensen.'

'Yes, yes, I know that,' snapped the chief constable impatiently. 'You told me that on the phone. But what's happened to Mr. Jensen?'

'He's dead, sir,' answered Inspector Rooper simply.

The major clicked his teeth sympathetically. 'How did it happen?' he asked, and his voice was appreciably lower.

'Well, it looks as if it had been an

accident, sir,' said the inspector. 'He was smothered under that pile of gravel.' He pointed to the heap of sand and stones that lay at the foot of the bank.

'Smothered under the gravel,' echoed the chief constable in astonishment. 'I don't understand what you mean. How did he get under the gravel?'

'That seems to be simple enough, sir,' replied Rooper. 'There were two cart-loads of gravel up on the top there,' he said, raising his head and looking up to the top of the bank, 'an' the wind must 'ave blown one of them over just as Mr. Jensen was passin' underneath.'

'How was the discovery made?' asked Trevor Lowe, who with White had been listening interestedly.

Inspector Rooper hesitated for a moment before answering the question of a stranger, but since Lowe had come with the chief constable, he apparently came to the conclusion that it was all right. 'Some workmen found the body this morning, sir,' he said. 'They haven't been working here for the past two days on account of the storm, but this mornin', it 'aving cleared up, they arrived as usual at seven. Tom Porch 'ere —' He jerked his thumb towards the little group by the heap of gravel, and a thickset labourer, hearing his name, stepped forward. ' — 'e found the overturned cart of gravel.'

'That's right.' Tom Porch took a part in the conversation with evident relish. 'I seed that this wind 'ad blown the cart over and shot the gravel down onter the road, so I thought as we'd best start by clearin' it up. Garge and me tackled it right away, and we 'adn't bin on the job long afore we found the body — lying right under the 'eap, it were.' Mr. Porch punctuated the account of his discovery with several nods of the head and much gusto, his mind no doubt full of the vista of free beer that loomed ahead. The relating of that story at the Rose and Crown would be worth many pints in the near future.

'Was he dead when you found him?' asked the dramatist.

'Aye, 'e were that,' replied Mr. Porch with considerable pride, as though he were personally responsible for the fact. 'I've never seen a deader.'

'What did you do then?' said Lowe.

'I sent Garge to the perlice station on his bicycle,' answered the man.

'It seems simple enough,' put in Major Strickland. 'Poor Jensen. What a horrible death!'

'Horrible,' agreed the dramatist. 'Do you mind if I have a look at the body?'

The chief constable looked at him a little doubtfully. 'I haven't any objection if you want to,' he said after a pause, 'although I don't see what — '

'It's got to do with me,' said Lowe with a smile. 'Well, as a matter of fact, I suppose it's got nothing, but ever since the Carraway affair and that business at Phantom Hollow, I've been rather interested in this kind of thing.'

'But this is completely different,' protested Major Strickland. 'This is an accident — '

'You don't know what it is yet, Strickland,' broke in Lowe. 'On the face of it, I agree it looks like a clear case of accidental death; but there's no harm in making sure.'

Major Strickland shrugged his shoulders.

It was obvious from the expression on his face that in his opinion his friend was trying to make a mountain out of a mole-hill.

Lowe walked over and bent down beside the still form that lay close up against the bank. The dead man was of massive build, with a strong face deeply scored with lines, and his dark hair was plentifully streaked with grey.

The dramatist put his age at about forty-five and learned later that he was only two years out in his judgment. Elmer N. Jensen was within three months of forty-seven when he died. There were distinct signs that his death had been the result of suffocation. His face was congested, his tongue swollen, and his eyes distended and suffused with blood.

The falling gravel must have stunned him, otherwise a man of his obvious strength would have found no difficulty in wriggling himself free. He was dressed in a brown lounge suit, and over this he wore a heavy fleecy overcoat. The cap he had been wearing still lay beside the body.

'It seems clear enough,' muttered Trevor Lowe, frowning. 'I wonder where he could have been going to or coming from when it happened? Where does this road lead to?'

'Straight across the open moor this way, sir,' answered Inspector Rooper. 'T'other way through Blackbarrow Coombe to the village.'

'Are there any other houses further along?' inquired the dramatist.

The inspector shook his grizzled head. 'No, nuthin' until you get to Black Tor, fifteen mile away,' he replied.

'There's the Black Moor Inn,' said the constable, speaking for the first time.

Rooper gave a contemptuous snort. 'Nobody 'ud want to go there,' he declared, 'least of all Mr. Jensen.'

'And would it be possible that Mr. Jensen had been down to the village and was returning home?' suggested Lowe.

'He wouldn't have to come anywhere near here to get to Ridgeway Manor from the village,' said the chief constable. 'You turn off before entering Blackbarrow Coombe.'

Trevor Lowe pursed his lips. 'The only thing that seems to me peculiar,' he said thoughtfully, 'is what he was doing walking

25

along this road that doesn't lead anywhere in a storm such as we had last night. No sane man would have gone out at all unless it was something urgent.'

'He was an American gentleman, sir,' said Inspector Rooper, as if that explained every form of peculiarity.

The dramatist smiled. 'Even American gentlemen don't stroll about aimlessly in rain and sleet with a gale of wind strong enough to blow the roof off,' he remarked. 'Still, why he was out and where he was going is probably none of our business.'

He had been gazing steadily at the body while he was speaking. Now he suddenly started, and, bending forward, peered closely at the brogue shoes with narrowed eyes.

'I evidently spoke too soon,' he exclaimed. His voice had taken on an inflexion that Arnold White recognized only too well. 'Everything that he did or ever has done will be our business.'

'What the devil do you mean?' demanded Major Strickland.

'Look at the soles of his shoes, man,' cried Lowe. 'Do you see — caked with cigarette ash. Jensen never walked to that pile of gravel at all. He was either carried there or brought in some vehicle.'

'Good God!' exclaimed the startled chief constable. 'Then it wasn't an accident?'

'No,' snapped Trevor Lowe, and his voice was grim. 'It was murder!'

3

The Green Pebble

The little group stared in open-mouthed amazement at Trevor Lowe and remained, so staring, in silence for nearly a minute after he had made his unexpected announcement.

Inspector Rooper was the first to break the silence. 'I don't see 'ow you can be sure, sir — ' he began doubtfully.

'I'm absolutely sure,' the dramatist said. 'It's obvious Jensen never walked along this road at all, or at least not when the gravel fell. If he had, with the road soaked with water as it was last night, that cigarette ash would have never remained on the soles of his shoes. It would have been washed off before he had gone two yards. He had trodden in cigarette ash that had been scattered on the floor or carpet of some building, and he never came out of that building on his feet. And I don't think we can argue against it.

It's a clear case of murder.'

'Well, that puts a different complexion on things,' said Inspector Hooper, scratching his head. 'But I don't see, if what you say is true, sir, 'ow 'e got under the gravel at all.'

'He got under the gravel,' said Lowe, 'because he was laid under the bank, and the gravel tipped on the top of him. It's one of the most ingenious schemes that ever went wrong.'

'Do you think that his death was actually the result of suffocation from the gravel?' said the chief constable. 'That he was alive when it was shot over him?'

'That I can't tell you,' said the dramatist. 'Probably a doctor would know, but I should think it was quite probable. Undoubtedly death was due to suffocation, but whether it was actually the gravel or whether he was suffocated first by some other means, I shouldn't like to say.'

'Whoever killed him seems to have gone to a lot of unnecessary trouble,' muttered the major.

'A lot of trouble, certainly, but I don't agree with you that it was unnecessary,' said

Lowe. 'The murderer or murderers took the greatest pains to make Jensen's death look like the result of an accident, and they very nearly succeeded.'

'It's a shocking business,' grunted Major Strickland, shaking his head. 'Poor fellow. It's bad enough if it had been an accident, but — murder ... ' He made a grimace and turned to the inspector. 'Have you notified them at Ridgeway Manor yet?'

'No, sir,' answered Rooper. 'I was waiting for the doctor to come along first.'

'Macaulay?'

The inspector nodded. 'Yes, I telephoned 'im the same time as I telephoned you, sir — from the station directly I 'eard the news, but Dr. Macaulay was out, seein' an urgent patient. I left word where I'd gone and asked him to follow as soon as 'e came 'ome.'

'Then I suppose we had better wait for his verdict before we communicate with the house,' said Strickland, his ruddy face paler than when he had left the Rose and Crown. 'It's going to be an unpleasant job breaking the news to his daughter.'

'Surely she must guess there's something wrong by now,' said Trevor Lowe, glancing at his watch. 'They would have missed him at breakfast and discovered that he hadn't been home all night.'

'Yes.' The chief constable puffed out his cheeks with a breath of relief. 'That may soften the blow a bit.'

'In the meanwhile,' suggested the dramatist, 'while we're waiting for Dr. Macaulay, we might have a look round here and see if there are any traces that will help us to identify the killer.'

Inspector Rooper looked a little annoyed. 'I think you can safely leave that in my 'ands, sir,' he said stiffly, regarding Lowe with a glance of disfavour. Who the devil was this man who was calmly butting in on his legitimate job?

'That's all right, Rooper,' put in Major Strickland hastily. 'This gentleman is a friend of mine, Mr. Trevor Lowe. He's had quite a good bit of experience at this sort of work, so I'm sure you won't object to letting him have a look round with you.'

'It's rather a hobby of mine,' said Lowe tactfully, 'and I should be awfully obliged, Inspector, if you would just let me mess around and enjoy myself.'

The stony face of the inspector softened. 'I shall be very pleased, sir,' he said, and shook the hand that Lowe held out with one of his pleasantest smiles.

'That's splendid,' said the dramatist. 'And don't get annoyed with me if I make one or two suggestions. I'm only an amateur at this game, but I might be quite helpful.'

'If you can help me, sir,' said Rooper, 'I'll be only too grateful. 'Ave you anything to suggest as a start, sir?'

'Only that we go carefully over the ground in the vicinity of the body,' said the dramatist, 'and then if it's possible to get to the top of this embankment, have a look at the overturned cart.'

The inspector agreed to this plan, and, while the two workmen looked on, the rest of the party began a thorough search of the ground round the heap of gravel. Every inch of the road for the space of ten yards on either side was subjected to the closest scrutiny; but whatever traces there may have been, the boots of the labourers and the police themselves had obliterated.

Only one piece of definite information resulted, and that was that Jensen had not been brought to the scene of his death in any form of vehicle. With the exception of the car in which they had come, there were no marks of tyres or wheels.

'It doesn't help us very much,' remarked the chief constable when Lowe drew his attention to this fact.

'Not very much, but it certainly helps,' said the dramatist.

'How?' demanded Major Strickland.

'Elmer Jensen was a heavy man,' said Lowe. 'Whoever carried him here couldn't have carried him very far. So obviously he was brought from somewhere that is not more than a mile away. That narrows down the location of the place we have to look for considerably. If he'd been brought here in a car or similar vehicle, he might have come from anywhere.'

The chief constable nodded. 'That's true,' he answered. 'And there aren't many houses within a radius of a mile from here.'

'Precious few,' said Inspector Rooper. 'There's Bellis, the keeper's, cottage.' He ticked them off on his fingers as he spoke. 'An' there's Mr. Sedgwick's place. Then there's the Black Moor Inn and the

Western's house. I think that's about all, 'cept for one or two shelters and barns.'

'And we mustn't leave those out of our calculations,' said Trevor Lowe. 'A barn or a shelter would fit as well as a house, possibly better, for people do not as a rule scatter cigarette ash about the floors of their houses. However, a visit to all the places you have mentioned, Inspector, can be carried out later. The next move, I think, is to have a look at that overturned cart.'

This turned out to be easier said than done, for it necessitated a walk of nearly half a mile before the embankment sloped sufficiently gently to be climbable. The inspector, however, possessed long legs, and could put on a good pace when he liked — and just at present he did like, so that very soon they had reached their objective and stood by the overturned cart, looking down at the others in the roadway below.

An inspection of the cart that had contained the gravel showed that it would have been the work of but a few seconds to have tipped the contents over the edge of the bank. It was one of those carts that tip up on the withdrawal of a pin, and this is exactly what had been done. It had not been overturned in the true sense of the word.

'That's the second mistake of our murderer,' said Lowe when he discovered this. 'And even without the ash, this would prove that the fall of that gravel was no accident. However fierce the wind was blowing, it couldn't pull out an iron pin.'

He searched the ground round the cart, but the long, rank grass showed no traces. On a frayed piece of ironwork that bound the wood of the cart itself, however, he did find something — a shred of grey wool. He showed it to the inspector, and Rooper carefully detached it and placed it in his notebook.

'I should think that had come from some article of clothing like an overcoat,' Lowe remarked. 'It's not much use to us now, but it may be very valuable later on — unless you happen to know anybody who wears a grey tweed overcoat?'

Rooper screwed up his eyes in concentration, but finally shook his head.

'I can't call anyone to mind at the moment,' he said, and at that moment they heard the chug-chug of a motor engine from the road below.

Peering down, Lowe saw that a dilapidated two-seater Ford had driven up, and its solitary occupant, a tall, thin man with a reddish moustache, was getting out.

'That's Dr. Macaulay,' said Inspector Rooper at his elbow.

'Then as there's nothing more to be learnt up here,' said the dramatist, 'wouldn't it be as well if we got back and heard what Dr. Macaulay has to say?'

They began to retrace their steps to the point from which they had ascended to the embankment.

'As soon as you've disposed of the doctor,' said Lowe, 'I think it would be a good idea to go along to Ridgeway and interview Jensen's household, don't you? It's more than likely that we shall learn something there. The first thing to establish is a motive for the crime.'

'There's plenty of those,' remarked Rooper, to the dramatist's surprise.

'Plenty of motives?' said Lowe. 'What do you mean?'

'What I say, sir,' answered the inspector.

'I could name at least four people who would have been glad to know Mr. Jensen was out of the way. That's why I sent for the major when I 'eard 'e was dead. I wasn't surprised to learn that it was no accident.'

'Who are your four suspects?' asked Trevor Lowe quickly.

'Well, they ain't exactly suspects,' replied Rooper, choosing his words with care. 'And with the exception of one, I don't think any of 'em 'ud go to the length of murder. I only said they'd be glad to know that Mr. Jensen was dead.'

'And who are the four people who would be glad to know that Jensen was dead?' asked the dramatist interestedly.

'Well, there's Mr. Leyton — Mr. John Leyton. 'E's the son of Sir Gordon Leyton, from whom Mr. Jensen bought Ridgeway. Sir Gordon went smash over some company or other up in Lunnon that Mr. Jensen was connected with and lost all 'is money. Young Mr. Leyton took the job of secretary to Mr. Jensen because 'e 'ad to live, but it's common knowledge round these parts that 'e 'ated him like poison because 'e was the cause of his father's smash. Then there's Jim

Box, o' the Black Moor Inn.'

The inspector paused while he climbed down onto the road.

"'E threatened to do the most 'orrible things to Mr. Jensen after Mr. Jensen thrashed him in the 'igh street fer trying ter kiss old Wyler's daughter when 'e was drunk. 'E's the one I was thinkin' of when I made that exception. I wouldn't put murder past Jim Box.'

'Go on,' said Lowe interestedly when Rooper stopped. 'That's two. Who are the other two?'

'Sedgwick's one of 'em,' replied the inspector. "'E's a writer chap — lives at Pine Cottage on the Ridgeway estate. I was walkin' 'ome one night through Blackbarrow Cobe, and I 'eard 'im and Mr. Jensen quarrelling something awful. I don't know what it was about, but I 'eard Sedgwick say: 'One day I'll kill you for that!' '

'Humph!' remarked Trevor Lowe. 'It doesn't sound as if Jensen had been particularly popular. Well, there's one more you haven't mentioned. Who's that?'

The inspector hesitated reluctantly. 'I don't s'pose you'll believe me,' he said.

'You'll think I'm mad.'

'At any rate, give me the chance,' said Lowe with a smile as his companion stopped abruptly.

'You understand that in this case I've got nothin' ter go on at all,' said Rooper, "cept the evidence of my own eyes.'

'Yes,' said the dramatist laconically. He was getting impatient.

'Well, then, sir,' said the inspector with a deep breath, 'the fourth one is his daughter!'

Trevor Lowe shot a sharp glance at the stolid face of the grizzled police officer, but it was expressionless. Lowe would have liked to ask him many questions, but as they had almost reached the group by the body he decided to defer them until later.

Dr. Macaulay had finished his examination, and was talking to the major when they came up. Strickland introduced Lowe, and the doctor nodded but made no audible comment.

'Well, what's the verdict?' asked the dramatist.

'There's na doot that Jensen was suffocated,' answered the doctor in a broad

Scottish accent. 'How he was suffocated I wudnae like ter say at the moment. Of course ye'll be havin' an autopsy?' He addressed the last remark to the chief constable.

Strickland nodded. 'Oh yes, we shall have to under the circumstances,' he replied.

'We might as well get the body to the mortuary,' broke in Inspector Rooper. 'Have you any objection to us using your car, sir?'

'Well — ' Major Strickland looked anything but pleased at the request.

'I'm sorry to ask, sir,' said the inspector, 'but the only ambulance we've got 'as got a wheel off.'

'In that case I suppose you'd better,' Strickland gave his consent grudgingly. 'I'll take you there and come back and pick up Mr. Lowe.'

'I can give Mistaire Lowe a lift back to the veelage,' said Dr. Macaulay.

'That's very good of you, Doctor,' said the dramatist with a smile. 'Thanks very much.'

The constable and Inspector Rooper were already lifting the limp form of Jensen, and as they moved it something dropped from the clothing. White darted forward and picked it up. With an exclamation of surprise he came over to them, holding out his find in the palm of his hand. It was a little grey-green stone about the size of a small walnut.

'What in the world is that?' said Major Strickland, staring at it with wrinkled brows.

'That's the most interesting thing we've found yet,' replied Trevor Lowe, taking it from his secretary and holding it between his forefinger and thumb.

'Do you *know* what it is?' asked the chief constable.

The dramatist nodded. *'Yes,'* he replied, 'that is an uncut diamond. Its value, I should say at a rough guess, is in the region of two hundred pounds!'

4

At Ridgeway Manor

Sitting in the charge-room of the little village police station, Trevor Lowe pondered over the mysterious problem presented by the murder of Elmer N. Jensen, while Inspector Rooper went about his duties connected with the routine work of the affair.

Here was a situation that at first glance seemed almost to defy solution, for the simple reason that there were, if Rooper was to be believed, so many possible solutions. Three people in that small community, it appeared, had almost equal interests in the death of the American. Lowe discounted the daughter, for if she were in any way guilty, it must have been indirectly. No woman could have carried out the crime as it had been carried out without an accomplice. But apart from her, there was the secretary, Leyton, who lived at Ridgeway Manor; Sedgwick, 'the writer chap', as

Rooper had described him; and Box of the Black Moor Inn. These last two had been heard to utter definite threats against the life of the murdered man. Obviously the first move was to inquire fully into the movements of these three and to seek, in the case of Sedgwick, the reason for those angrily uttered words that Inspector Rooper had overheard.

And then there was the little grey-green stone that Lowe had recognized as an uncut diamond. How did that fit into the business? Had robbery been the motive for Jensen's murder? It seemed peculiar if it had, for surely it was improbable that the American was in the habit of carrying about with him a collection of uncut diamonds. But perhaps the stone had not been Jensen's at all. Perhaps it had fallen from the murderer's pocket when he laid his victim down under the bank before tipping the gravel over him. It was all very involved, but Trevor Lowe was fascinated.

These sorts of problems held a strange appeal, and this one in particular. His return to London had been postponed indefinitely — indeed, he had sent White across to the Rose and Crown with instructions to countermand the cancelling of their rooms and to keep them on. There was something in the setting of the crime that appealed strongly to the dramatist's imagination — the twisting road winding up through Blackbarrow Coombe to the open moor, windswept by the full force of the gale.

He could picture the sinister figure of the murderer carrying his victim through the howling storm, the rain lashing round him, to that spot under the embankment; could picture him laying the unconscious form of Jensen down and then going along the road and up onto the embankment to release the pin that held the cart in place; and then, as the gravel rushed and slithered down, covering that silent figure beneath, stealing away into the storm and darkness, his work complete.

Or had there been more than one man? Had an accomplice looked after the tipping of the cart, while the other waited below to see the final touch put on his scheme? And from where had Jensen been brought in that unconscious state? From his own house in the valley; from Pine Cottage, the house of Sedgwick; from the lonely inn on the bleak moor; or from one of the innumerable shelters and barns that dotted the countryside? At present it was impossible to tell.

Lowe's train of thought was interrupted by the entrance of Inspector Rooper. 'I'm going along to Ridgeway now, sir,' he announced. 'Perhaps you'd care to come with me?'

'That's very nice of you, Inspector,' said Lowe. 'I should, very much. If you wait two or three minutes, I'll get my car and we can go in that.'

The inspector agreed, and Lowe left the little police station and walked across the road to the garage, where he had housed the Rolls, which was almost opposite. On the way he met White coming out of the Rose and Crown.

'I've fixed our rooms all right,' said his secretary, 'and now I'm going down to the post office to send a wire to Robins, telling him we shan't be back for a few days and asking him to send any letters on here.'

'Right you are,' answered Lowe. 'I'm going along with Inspector Rooper to

Ridgeway. I'll come back to the inn and meet you for lunch as soon as we've finished. In the meanwhile, you might have a chat with our friend the landlord and see what you can learn about Jensen, Sedgwick, Leyton and Jim Box. There's no one better than the landlord of the local hostel if you want to find out the truth about anyone.'

White nodded and went off to the post office, while Lowe entered the garage and got out his car. He picked up Rooper on the steps of the station, and then, following the inspector's directions, sent the car humming along the crisp road towards Ridgeway.

At the beginning of Blackbarrow Coombe, a private road branched sharply to the left, leading down a steep decline to the lodge gates, which were open. Lowe steered the car into a winding drive that ran between an avenue of tall beech trees. It twisted and turned for nearly three-quarters of a mile, and then they came in sight of the house. Ridgeway Manor was an imposing Elizabethan building of age-old, ivy-covered red brick set amongst trim lawns and backed by a thick woodland, against the interlaced branches of whose trees the tall, twisted chimneys stood out with picturesque effect.

Trevor Lowe brought the car to a halt in front of the pillared entrance, and he and the inspector got out and rang the wrought-iron bell-pull. Instead of the deep jangling that he had expected, Lowe heard the soft purr of an electric bell. Evidently modern improvements had been fitted at the manor either by Sir Gordon Leyton or the latest unfortunate owner.

After a very slight pause, the massive oak door was opened and an elderly man in the sombre garb of the upper servant appeared on the threshold. The anxious expression on his face deepened as he caught sight of, and obviously recognized, Inspector Rooper.

'Is Miss Jensen at home, Mr. Chayne?' asked the inspector politely.

The butler, for that was plainly the position he occupied in the household, inclined his head. 'Yes, Mr. Rooper,' he answered. 'Did you wish to see her?' And when the inspector nodded: 'Is it anything about the master?'

'Well, as a matter of fact, it is,' said Rooper hesitantly. 'I'm afraid I've brought some bad news.'

The butler looked even more depressed than when he had opened the door. 'I was afraid of it,' he muttered. 'What has happened to him?'

'He's been murdered,' replied the inspector bluntly.

Chayne's face went a sickly grey. 'Murdered!' he repeated, and after a long pause: 'If — if you'll come into the drawing room, I'll fetch Miss Dorothy.'

He ushered them into a large, pleasantly furnished room opening off the wide hall, and hurried away.

'Nasty business, this,' remarked the inspector, seating himself gingerly on the extreme edge of the least secure-looking chair in the room. 'I don't relish the idea of breaking the news at all.'

'So far as it is possible to tell from the butler's expression,' remarked Trevor Lowe, 'I don't think you'll find it requires much breaking.'

Rooper made no comment, and they waited in silence until they heard a quick footstep approaching. The inspector rose to greet the newcomer, but it was a man who entered the room and not the woman they were expecting. His age was in the region of twenty-eight, and he was fair-haired, with rather deep-set grey eyes that darted sharply from one to the other as he closed the door behind him.

'What's this you've been telling Chayne, Rooper?' he asked quickly.

'Mr. Jensen was murdered at some time during the night, Mr. Leyton,' answered the inspector, 'and his body was found early this morning on the Blackbarrow road.'

'Good God!' exclaimed the fair man. 'Murdered! So that's what happened to him, eh?'

'Were you expecting something to happen to him?' asked Trevor Lowe, eyeing the secretary keenly.

'Naturally,' replied Leyton, staring back at the dramatist, and evidently wondering who the deuce he was. 'As a matter of fact I've just been trying to phone through to the police station, but the confounded storm must have damaged the telephone connection. When we discovered that his bed hadn't been slept in, and he was nowhere to be found in the house, we got anxious.'

'Surely you were leaving it a trifle late to start inquiries?' said Lowe. 'It's nearly half-past twelve now.'

'We only discovered he was missing a quarter of an hour ago,' answered the secretary. 'Mr. Jensen was a very bad sleeper, and usually went to bed very late. For that reason he gave orders that he was never to be disturbed in the morning until he rang.'

'I see,' the dramatist said with a nod. 'How did you discover, then, that his bed hadn't been slept in?'

'I had some important documents that had to catch the midday collection,' was the reply, 'and before I could send them off they required Mr. Jensen's signature. I knew he was particularly anxious that they should go, and so for once I risked disturbing him. When I got no answer to my knocking, I tried the handle of his door and, to my surprise, found it unlocked.'

'I see,' said Lowe again.

'You say he was murdered?' Leyton addressed the remark to Inspector Rooper. 'How did it happen?'

'If you mean who killed 'im, Mr. Leyton,'

answered the inspector, 'I don't know. If you mean how did he die — well, he was suffocated.'

He briefly related the circumstances surrounding the finding of the body. Leyton listened interestedly.

'It's almost incredible,' he exclaimed when the inspector had finished. 'Not that Jensen should have been killed; I don't mean that — I'm surprised that somebody hasn't killed him long before now — but that it should have happened just in the way it did.'

'What do you mean by that, Mr. Leyton?' asked Lowe curiously.

'If you'd known Jensen, you wouldn't need to ask that,' retorted the secretary. 'He was far too fond of his own comfort to go out in a storm like we had here last night. The mystery to me is what he could have been doing on the Blackbarrow road at that time of night.'

'At what time of night?' said the dramatist sharply.

Leyton flushed. Whether or not it was at Lowe's sharpness of tone, it was impossible to say. 'Well, it must have been latish when he went out,' he answered. 'We didn't finish dinner until after eight.'

'Did Jensen dine with you?'

'Yes, but he asked for his coffee to be taken into his study. I understood he was going to work.'

'When was the last time you saw him — at dinner?' inquired the dramatist.

'Yes. He said good night to myself and Dor — his daughter, saying he probably wouldn't see us again that night as he'd got a lot to do.'

'Was he his usual self during dinner? Was there anything about his manner that differed in any way from his normal behaviour?'

By tacit consent, Inspector Rooper had subsided into the background and was letting Lowe do all the questioning.

'He was a little bit more disagreeable than usual, if that's what you mean,' replied Leyton shortly.

'That's partly what I mean, but not quite,' said Lowe with a slight smile. 'I'll put the question differently. Did he by any action or word lead you to suppose that he had anything on his mind — that he was, in short, going out to keep an appointment?'

The secretary shook his head. 'No — not then,' he said.

'When did he, then?' asked the dramatist.

'Well, there was a registered letter for him by the second post yesterday, and as it was marked personal, I gave it to him to open. He went very pale when he read it, and swore horribly. I didn't take much notice of the swearing part of it — that was quite a common occurrence — but he muttered something about 'choosing a filthy night like this'.'

Lowe's eyes narrowed. 'What happened to the letter?' he inquired.

'Jensen threw it on the fire.'

'And the envelope as well?'

'Yes.

'You didn't happen to notice the post-mark, I suppose?'

Leyton shook his head.

'Did Jensen have any dealings with diamonds?' asked the dramatist after a slight pause.

'No, not so far as I know,' replied the secretary.

'You've never seen anything like this

in his possession?' Lowe turned to the inspector. 'Have you that stone, Rooper?' he said.

The inspector nodded, and extracting the little grey-green stone from one of his waist-coat pockets, handed it to the dramatist. Lowe held it out for Leyton to see, and the secretary peered at it with wrinkled brows.

'No, never,' he declared.

Trevor Lowe passed the uncut diamond back to Rooper and tried another opening. 'Mr. Leyton,' he said, 'do you know of anything in connection with Mr. Jensen's life — past or present — that would be likely to throw any light on his mysterious death?'

Leyton hesitated. 'No,' he said slowly at length.

Lowe was convinced the man was keeping something back, but for the moment he didn't press his question, but adroitly followed it up with another. 'I am given to understand that Jensen and your father had business dealings together at one time,' he said. 'Is that true, Mr. Leyton?'

Leyton's face darkened, and his eyes clouded. 'Business dealings!' He laughed harshly. 'Some people would call them that, no doubt. Jensen ruined my father, and drove him to his death. If anybody ever rendered the world a service and rid it of the biggest scoundrel who ever existed, that person was the man who killed Elmer N. Jensen!'

5

The Second Crime

In the silence which followed young Leyton's sudden outburst, Trevor Lowe heard a light step pause outside the door, and then it opened and a woman came into the room.

She was slim, and because of her slimness looked taller than she really was. Her small, well-shaped head was crowned with sleek fair hair that gleamed in the light of the window. An attractive woman, thought Lowe, pretty but not beautiful — the nose was slightly too small, the eyes slightly too far apart, the red mouth slightly too large for real beauty. But undeniably attractive. He waited for her to speak, expecting, since her father had been an American, to hear the usual nasal twang.

'Chayne has just told me the news,' she said calmly, and the dramatist received a shock, for her voice was low and slightly husky, but without the smallest trace of an accent. He noted, too, that there was no sign of sorrow on her face as she spoke. Her cheeks were a trifle paler than they should have been, and her lips in repose were rather tightly pressed together, but that was all.

'You shouldn't have come in here, Dorothy,' exclaimed Leyton, 'and I told Chayne not to say anything.'

'Why?' she asked. 'I was bound to learn sooner or later.'

'Yes, but — ' began the secretary, when Lowe broke in.

'It is just as well that Miss Jensen is here,' he said. 'It's quite possible she may be able to help us.'

Dorothy turned her large violet-blue eyes towards him and looked at him steadily. 'How is it possible that I can help you?' she said slowly.

'You'll understand what I mean when you know exactly what has happened,' said Trevor Lowe, and as gently as possible he told her.

Her face remained perfectly expressionless throughout. Not the smallest trace of emotion ruffled its calm. From her outward appearance, Dorothy Jensen might have been listening to the story of something that had happened to a stranger.

'I still don't see how you expect me to be able to help you,' she said when the dramatist had finished.

'What we're looking for is some kind of motive,' explained Lowe. 'This was obviously no spur-of-the-moment crime. It had been carefully planned and premeditated. Now, if you know anything in your father's life that would give us a hint — '

'I know very little about his life,' she interrupted. 'He never made a confidant of anyone, least of all of me. I am quite prepared, however, to believe that there were scores of motives for his being murdered.'

Trevor Lowe felt a growing amazement at the cool way in which this woman was taking the news of the tragedy. What manner of man could Jensen have been to have inspired this almost universal hatred? Only on very few occasions during his life had he felt so completely nonplussed.

Dorothy was obviously trying to put him off. He was certain she knew more than she had said, and he was determined to try and discover what this was. 'Surely you must know something,' he urged, and proceeded to question her about the uncut diamond they had found under the body.

Like Leyton, however, Dorothy Jensen denied all knowledge of it. She declared that she had never seen it before, and was completely unaware that her father ever had such things in his possession. After a great deal of trouble — for she seemed reluctant to talk about the subject — the dramatist succeeded in eliciting the following meagre facts concerning Jensen's past life.

He had spent many years in America, partly in New York and partly in Chicago, during which time his daughter had been at a convent in France. When she was eighteen — four years ago — her father had turned up one day at the convent and taken her away. He had taken her to a large house at Golder's Green, where they had lived until he had bought and moved to Ridgeway.

Of his life prior to his coming and fetching her from the convent, she knew nothing, and beyond the fact that Jensen had seemed to be very rich, had not added anything to her knowledge since. She frankly admitted that she had disliked her father intensely, and this dislike had reached its height when she learned that he had practically swindled Sir Gordon Leyton out of most of his fortune. And that was about all the information Lowe could get.

Leyton was prepared to go into a rather more detailed account of his father's dealings with Jensen which, boiled down, resulted in the not uncommon story of an un-businesslike country gentleman who had been trying to increase his inadequate income being fleeced by a man who was not above a little legal sharp practice. Jensen had done nothing that could be called criminal, but he had rather taken advantage of the other's trustfulness and lack of business knowledge.

The loss of his money and the home he had lived in since he was a boy had brought on an illness from which he never recovered, and very shortly after Jensen took up his residence at Ridgeway, Sir Gordon Leyton had died. Jensen had offered the son a position as his secretary, which had been accepted; and although he had only seen them together for a few minutes, Trevor Lowe could have given a shrewd guess that the pleasure of living under the same roof as Dorothy Jensen had gone a long way towards John Leyton's acceptance of a job that he must have loathed.

Having learnt all there was to be learnt, or rather all they appeared likely to divulge, from the secretary and the dead man's daughter, Rooper turned his attention to the servants. But here again he met with an even blanker wall.

None of them had been in Jensen's employ longer than a year, and knew absolutely nothing that was the slightest degree helpful. No strangers had ever called to see Jensen, and the only resident in Stoneford who had ever been to Ridgeway was Sedgwick, the tenant of Pine Cottage.

An inspection of the papers in the dead man's study, which was conducted under the supervision of the secretary, was equally as futile. There were several documents connected with a number of companies in which he was interested, but no private letters, papers or diaries of any kind. Jensen's past was a sealed book that no amount of probing and questioning could unfasten.

'There's a chance you might learn something about him from the American police department, isn't there?' said Lowe, as he and Inspector Rooper drove slowly back towards the lodge gates. 'So far as there's anything to be found out about him there, he might have been born yesterday.'

Rooper nodded. 'I'm getting an inquiry put through to America at once,' he said. 'Unless we can pick up some more evidence before, I shall ask at the inquest for an adjournment.'

'How far away are we from Sedgwick's place?' asked Trevor Lowe as the car turned out of the private road into Blackbarrow Coombe.

'Not very far,' answered the inspector. 'About half a mile up the coombe, and then a hundred yards down a narrow lane on the right. Why, sir?'

'I thought it wouldn't be a bad idea to call on him,' said the dramatist, 'after what you told me you overheard. And afterwards we could go along and have a chat with Box.'

'If they don't know any more than the

people at Ridgeway, we shan't be much better off,' grunted Rooper.

'If they don't say any more, you mean,' corrected Trevor Lowe.

The inspector glanced at him sideways. 'Why, do you think they know more than they've said, sir?' he asked.

'I do. In fact, I'm sure that both Leyton and Miss Jensen could have given us a lot more information if they'd liked.'

'It struck me a bit like that, too, sir,' admitted Rooper.

'And those papers in the study — did you notice anything about them?'

'The papers, sir?' The inspector thought for a moment and then shook his head. 'No, sir, I can't say I did. There weren't many, were there?'

'That's exactly what I mean,' said the dramatist. 'There weren't enough, Rooper, even for a secretive man. I think those papers had been carefully gone over long before we arrived at Ridgeway.'

'By Mr. Leyton, do you mean?' exclaimed the astonished inspector.

'By Leyton or Miss Jensen, or both,' said Lowe with conviction. 'I'm pretty sure the servants are quite open and straightforward.'

Inspector Rooper drew a long breath. 'Well, it does seem to be a bit of a puzzle, sir, don't it?'

'It does more than seem; it is. Is this the lane you mentioned?' He drew up the car opposite a narrow track that was half-hidden by the branches of the hedges that grew sprawlingly on either side.

'That's it, sir,' said Rooper. 'The gate leading to Pine Cottage is about halfway down.'

'We can't take the car along there,' remarked Lowe. 'We shall have to leave it here and walk.' Suiting the action to the word, he shut off the engine and got down, followed by Rooper.

Together they made their way along the narrow lane, which was little better than a footpath, until it widened out into a crescent-shaped clearing. Set in the hedge at this point was a wooden gate, and beyond the gate could be seen a low thatch-roofed cottage with a background of the trees that evidently gave it its name.

Trevor Lowe lifted the latch and walked

up the crazy pavement of the little front garden. A latticed porch enclosed the door, and pausing until the inspector reached his side, the dramatist raised his hand and gave a sharp rat-tat on the rusty knocker. The sound echoed hollowly, but though they waited for some time, nobody came in answer.

'He's out, I expect,' said Rooper. 'Mr. Sedgwick's a rare one fer walkin' in all weathers.'

Lowe knocked again, louder and longer, but there was no reply. 'I think we're wasting time,' he murmured. 'He must be out, as you say.'

He was in the act of turning away when something on the cracked step under his feet caught his eye. 'Just a moment, Inspector,' he said in a curiously altered voice. Stooping, he laid his finger on a small dark stain close up against the bottom of the door. When he removed it, it was wet and sticky and streaked with crimson. 'There's something wrong here,' he snapped. 'That's blood!'

Before Rooper could frame the words that were trembling on his lips, the dramatist had flung himself bodily at the front door. The flimsy lock parted under his weight and the door crashed open with a bang.

'You shouldn't have done that, sir,' began Rooper, his official instincts aroused. 'We've no right —'

He broke off, glaring at the crumpled thing that lay face upwards in the narrow passage. A little dark stream had collected around it, and the black hilt of a knife protruded from the breast.

'Good God!' gasped the inspector huskily. 'It's Mr. Sedgwick!'

Trevor Lowe bent down and gently touched the cold face. 'He's one of your suspects that you can cross off the list, Inspector,' he said soberly. 'He's dead!'

6

The Link

'As near as I can tell,' said Dr. Macaulay, rising to his feet and addressing Trevor Lowe and Inspector Rooper, 'he's been dead for about seven hours.'

The dramatist glanced at his watch. 'That would put the time of the murder at approximately half-past six this morning,' he said.

The doctor nodded gravely. 'About that,' he agreed. 'I wudnae like to be certain to an hour.'

After the discovery of the dead man in the hall of Pine Cottage, the inspector had volunteered to go back to the village in Lowe's car and fetch Dr. Macaulay, leaving the dramatist to guard all that was left of Sedgwick.

Rooper had served in a motor transport corps during the war, and the powerful Rolls therefore presented no difficulties to him.

He had been gone less than twenty minutes, and during that time Lowe had made a close examination of the path leading up to the front door, and also of the road outside the little gate, in the hope of finding some clue to the murderer; but the hard, frosty ground yielded no traces whatsoever.

The knife with which the deed had been committed was also valueless as a clue. It was a very ordinary knife, of the kind that are sold by hundreds to gardeners, labourers, and such-like, and was not even new. There was, of course, the possibility that there might be fingerprints on the black bone handle, and with this idea in view it had been carefully wrapped up by Inspector Rooper after the doctor had completed his examination, for the purpose of testing. But Trevor Lowe had little hope that anything would be discovered.

'It's a very strange affair,' remarked Dr. Macaulay as he prepared to depart. 'The veelage seems to have become the centre of dark happenings. Will you be thinkin' that this crime has any connection with the death of Mr. Jensen?'

'It's impossible to say definitely,' answered

Trevor Lowe cautiously. 'Personally I should say there was a very close connection. Sedgwick knew Jensen very well, and was, I believe, one of the few people who used to visit Ridgeway Manor. If this murder has nothing whatever to do with the death of Jensen, then it's the most extraordinary coincidence I've ever come across. At the same time, there's always the possibility that it may be a coincidence, and one has to bear that in mind.'

'It'll cause a panic in the veelage,' said Macaulay, shaking his head. 'There'll be few people who will venture out from their homes after dark, and I for one will not be blaming them. It's a terribly disturbing thought, Mr. Lowe, that there's a killer loose round the neighbourhood. One begins to wonder who's likely to be the next victim.'

'You can take it from me, Doctor,' said the dramatist, 'that if there are going to be any more victims, they have already been marked down. These two crimes are not haphazard ones. They are part of a carefully woven pattern, with a strong motive behind. No one has anything to fear unless they themselves are pieces of that pattern.'

'It's very disconcerting, all the same,' said Dr. Macaulay. 'What could the motive be, do you think?'

'I haven't the least idea,' replied the dramatist candidly. 'I should imagine that it will be necessary to institute a close search into the past lives of both the dead men before we are likely to discover that.'

'You think we shall learn something by that, sir?' said the inspector.

'I should think it would be quite probable,' answered Lowe. 'Tell me — how long has Sedgwick lived here?'

'Just on a year, sir,' said Rooper. 'He came to the cottage about a month after Mr. Jensen moved into the manor.'

'Yes, that would be about the time,' agreed the doctor. 'I bought poor old Dr. Walker's practice just round about then, too.'

'So Sedgwick and Jensen practically came to Stoneford together, did they?' murmured Trevor Lowe. 'That's a point worth noting and remembering.'

The inspector looked at him as though he would have liked to ask a question, but remained silent.

'Weel,' said Dr. Macaulay, picking up his little black bag, 'I'll be getting back. There are one or two patients I have to see.' He chuckled. 'Patients are not too numerous roond these parts, Mr. Lowe, and the few I have must be treated with reespect.'

He refused Lowe's suggestion that the inspector should drive him to the village with the remark that the walk would do him good, and when he had gone the dramatist turned briskly to Rooper.

'Now, Inspector,' he said, 'I think the next move is a complete search of this cottage and the dead man's effects.'

Rooper nodded. 'Yes, sir,' he agreed; 'and I hope we shall find something more than we did in the other case.'

'What I'm hoping you will find,' said Trevor Lowe, 'is some connection between Sedgwick and Jensen. There *was* some connection, Inspector, and it appears to have been a very extraordinary one.'

'How do you mean, sir?'

'Well, one could hardly call it friendly. After the words you heard Sedgwick utter to Jensen, it would seem that there was a decided enmity between them, on

71

Sedgwick's side at any rate, and yet he was a constant visitor at the manor. It would be fairly reasonable to suppose that Sedgwick was blackmailing Jensen but for two facts, both of which are directly opposed to that theory.'

'Which two are you referring to, sir?' said Rooper, whose mind was at the moment reeling with facts, none of which seemed to have any resemblance to common sense.

'Firstly,' said Trevor Lowe, 'the words Sedgwick used to Jensen in the lane: 'One day I'll kill you for that.' If Jensen had been the person to utter that threat, the theory that Sedgwick was blackmailing him would be tenable, but they are certainly not the words a blackmailer would be expected to use to his victim. The last thing a blackmailer wants is for his victim to die. The demise of the goose that lays the golden eggs would be a tragedy. Secondly, if Jensen were still alive and Sedgwick were the only dead man in the affair, the thing would be easy, for then we have a motive. Sedgwick blackmails Jensen. Jensen gets tired of being bled, and kills him. But Jensen is killed too, and if Dr. Macaulay is right, Jensen was killed first.'

'Mightn't it 'ave been possible that Jensen was blackmailing Sedgwick?' suggested the inspector.

Lowe shook his head. 'Not only do the same difficulties arise with that theory,' he said, 'but fresh ones as well. It doesn't fit in with the fact that both of them are dead. If you take blackmail as the connection between Sedgwick and Jensen, then who was the third person who murdered them, and why?'

Inspector Rooper frowned and scratched his grizzled head. 'It's a rare licker,' he declared. 'I can't see daylight anywhere.'

'Well, let's get on with our search,' said Trevor Lowe with a smile. 'It may not exactly flood the case with daylight, but there's a chance it will provide us with a feeble substitute.'

There were only four rooms in Pine Cottage, and one of these did duty as a kitchen, though it was so small that there was scarcely room for anything more than the table and two chairs it contained. The other three consisted of the main sitting room, which opened off the little hall; a smaller room, which led from it; and a bedroom, which was at the back of the house behind the sitting room. There was no upper part, the cottage having been built on the lines of the modern bungalow.

Trevor Lowe and the inspector began their investigations in the sitting room. It was sparsely furnished. An old-fashioned gate-legged table occupied the centre, and a worn and springless settee and easy-chair were drawn up to the fireplace. Beyond these articles and a sideboard, there was little else. Not a very comfortable place in which to live, was Lowe's mental comment as he surveyed the room, and certainly as yet no evidence of Sedgwick's alleged literary occupations.

An oil lamp stood on the table, and open by it was a cheap edition of a popular novel, but that was the only sign of any books or papers in the room. It struck Lowe as a significant fact that the oil lamp was still alight. It had therefore been burning all night, and the body in the hall had been fully clothed. Sedgwick, then, had not been to bed.

The dramatist's keen eyes spotted a pair

of boots by the hearth, and he picked them up. The soles were thickly caked with mud — mud that was still damp to the touch. Sedgwick had apparently been out during that night of storm, and when he had returned had changed his boots for the shoes in which he had met his death. Whose hand had knocked on that front door just after dawn and brought him out into the grey hall?

Lowe put the boots down with the question unanswered, and with the help of the inspector began to examine the drawers in the sideboard. One contained some odd bits of string, a few corks, a corkscrew, and a screwdriver; nothing else. In the other they found a writing pad, a packet of envelopes, and a small bottle of ink. Lowe looked for the blotting-paper in the writing pad, but it had been torn out.

At the extreme back of the drawer was a small cardboard box, and this the dramatist opened. He was usually good at suppressing any outward signs of emotion, but at sight of the contents he couldn't help the sudden exclamation that passed his lips. Lying in a piece of cotton wool were two grey-green stones: uncut diamonds, identical — except that they were slightly larger — to the one found under the dead body of Elmer N. Jensen!

7

The Unknown Strikes Again

'Well, that finally establishes a connection between the two crimes!' said Trevor Lowe as Inspector Rooper and he gazed down at the stones that the dramatist had tipped out of the box into the palm of his hand. 'There wasn't much doubt before, but the finding of these clinches it.'

'I don't understand it at all,' declared the puzzled inspector. 'If these 'ere stones belonged to Jensen, 'ow do they come to be in the possession of Sedgwick? And if they was the motive for the murders, why didn't the murderer take them away with 'im?'

'I can't tell you any more than you know,' said Trevor Lowe. 'For all we know, these diamonds may be the legitimate property of Sedgwick, and the one found under Jensen's body may have been given him by Sedgwick to sell. It sounds unconvincing, and I don't say it's the correct explanation, but it's impossible to theorize without anything to theorize on. We haven't got sufficient data yet.'

He put the two little grey-green pebbles back in the box and gave it into Rooper's charge. 'Let's go on with our search and see if we can find anything else,' he went on. 'One thing is certain — Sedgwick may have told people round here that he was engaged in literary work, but that was obviously untrue. There are no signs of his having been engaged in anything of the sort.'

'He was supposed to be writing a novel,' said Rooper. 'That's what he told Crampton, the postmaster.'

'It was certainly a blind. There's nothing here he could have written it on unless we find something in one of the other rooms. Only about three sheets of that writing pad have been used.'

They continued their examination of the sitting room, but found nothing else of interest. In the cupboard of the sideboard were two full bottles of whisky and one that was half-empty, three siphons, and half a dozen glasses, but that was all. They passed through into the smaller room adjoining.

This contained no furniture at all, and, except for three suitcases and an American trunk, was empty. Sedgwick appeared to have done a considerable amount of travelling, for the suitcases were plastered all over with labels. One of these attracted Lowe's attention, and he pointed it out to the inspector.

'So Sedgwick, too, had been to America,' he remarked softly. 'That is yet another link between him and Jensen. It would be interesting to know if they had been out there together.'

'You mean that something that occurred out in America may be the motive at the bottom of these murders?' said Rooper with a burst of intelligence.

'Exactly. And if they were associated in New York or Chicago, and we can discover who else was associated with them, we shall probably have gone a long way towards giving a name to the person who killed them.'

'In the meanwhile, we may as well have a look through these things,' said the inspector, indicating the suitcases and the trunk. 'Perhaps there are some papers or something.'

The suitcases yielded nothing but a few discarded clothes and some shirts and collars. But the American trunk proved a little more helpful. It was locked, but they found the right key on the bunch they had taken from Sedgwick's pocket and opened it. Several suits of clothes were hung in orderly array on the hangers provided for that purpose, and in the pocket of a blue serge jacket Lowe discovered a dirty piece of crumpled paper. Smoothing it out carefully, he saw that it was covered with lines of pencilled writing, and after a great deal of trouble he succeeded in deciphering the message. It ran:

'G. will take them all, I think, and no questions asked. I am arranging appointment for you to see him next week. Bring specimens with you.'

There was no signature, date or address. Trevor Lowe read it through again slowly and frowned. Who was G., and what did 'them all' refer to? The most obvious solution was the diamonds. No doubt the two Lowe had found in the cardboard box were the specimens that Sedgwick was to bring. This seemed to indicate that there were more of them somewhere. Or had the appointment with the mysterious G. been kept, and the rest of the uncut stones sold? It was hardly likely, because in that case surely the other two would have gone as well. It was much more likely that the appointment hadn't been kept, or that G. had, after all, refused to buy the stones.

Lowe talked it over with the inspector, but they arrived at no very satisfactory conclusion. As a clue, the pencilled message seemed useless. It was impossible to trace the writer, and there were so many people whose initial was G. in the world that it would be hopeless trying to find out to whom it referred.

'The trouble with this case, sir,' said the inspector in a rather aggrieved voice, 'is that there ain't nothing to go on. There's a lot of stray bits and pieces, as you might say, but nothing that makes sense.'

Lowe heartily agreed with him.

'However,' he said later, when a constable had arrived to take charge of the place, and he and Inspector Rooper prepared to take their leave, having completed a thorough search without finding anything else of interest, 'all we can do is to hope for the best. Something is bound to turn up sooner or later, and I am relying on you getting some useful information from America regarding Sedgwick's and Jensen's pasts. I feel confident that the core of the whole mystery lies there.'

He dropped Rooper at the police station and went across to the Rose and Crown. White was just sitting down to a belated lunch, having given up Lowe, and during the meal the dramatist acquainted him with the latest developments. White listened with interest.

'It rather complicates matters, doesn't it?' he commented when the dramatist concluded.

'In one way it does,' answered Lowe, 'and in another it doesn't. Before, when it was only Jensen's murder we were investigating, anybody might have been the culprit. There were any number of motives for killing him, so far as one could glean. Now, however, we are able to narrow down the motive to something that must also embrace a reason for killing Sedgwick. So to a certain extent it's going to make our search for the motive a little easier.'

He pushed his soup plate aside and helped himself to the appetizing cutlets that had been placed before him. 'How did you get on?' he inquired when the beaming waitress had departed. 'Did you learn anything about Jensen?'

White made a wry face. 'Not much, I'm afraid. I had a chat with the landlord here, and except that Jensen appears to have been thoroughly disliked in the village, he seemed to know very little about him.'

'What was the reason for this general dislike of the man? Did he tell you?'

'Yes; it seems that the inhabitants of Stoneford rather resent the way he treated Sir Gordon Leyton. It leaked out that Jensen was responsible for ruining the old man, and the villagers have never forgiven him for it. The Leytons have lived at Ridgeway Manor for centuries, and become almost as much a part of the place as the moors. The landlord says they don't take kindly to strangers in these parts.'

'What about the rest of the household at Ridgeway?' asked Lowe. 'How do they look upon the daughter?'

'Quite favourably, so far as I can make out. But that may be because it seems that local gossip has linked her name with John Leyton.'

'Ah!' remarked Lowe, nodding. 'So I was right. I thought this morning that that was the way the wind was blowing. Is there anything like a formal engagement between them?'

White shook his head. 'I couldn't say. The landlord says they're always about together.'

'I see.' Lowe crumbled his bread. 'Well, she's a very attractive woman, and Leyton's by no means ill-looking, so I shouldn't be surprised if under the circumstances the inevitable had happened. Whether they're engaged or not is immaterial. I shall certainly have to have another talk with both of them, because I'm sure they know more than they've said. They're both concealing something, and I want to know what it is.'

'The man who seems to have had the greatest motive for killing Jensen is the innkeeper, Box,' said White. 'Jensen apparently thrashed him almost to a state of unconsciousness, and when Box recovered he swore he'd get even with him, even if he swung for it. The landlord says the man has got a terrible temper, and when he's drunk is capable of anything.'

'Maybe,' answered Lowe. 'But this Jensen murder wasn't the work of a drunken man or of a man in a temper. It was cold-blooded and calculating. Besides, there's no reason why Box should have killed Sedgwick, and I'm certain the two crimes have the same basic motive.'

They continued to discuss the problem until they had finished their coffee, but in the end were no further advanced than when they had started. Here were two murders perpetrated within a few hours of each other; and the murderer had got away without, at the moment, leaving the smallest clue that was likely to lead to his identity being discovered.

For most of that afternoon Trevor Lowe turned the affair over in his mind, striving to reduce the meagre pieces of information he had succeeded in picking up to a coherent pattern. But nothing fitted.

It was all wrong. The words uttered by Sedgwick and overheard by Rooper pointed to Sedgwick as being Jensen's murderer, but the man had been murdered himself. To whom did the uncut diamonds belong, Sedgwick or Jensen? How did they come into the business, and who had sent that registered letter that had apparently been the cause of Jensen's journey on that stormy night which had ended in his death?

What had the letter contained? Evidently some kind of an appointment that Jensen for some reason or other had felt bound to keep. That was the only explanation for his remark when he had opened it, unless the secretary had been lying, and there had never been a registered letter at all. That was a possibility that had to be taken into consideration. Lowe decided to test it at once. The post office, which was also a general store, was only a stone's throw from the Rose and Crown, and he put on his hat and sallied forth to make the inquiry.

The postmaster was most voluble. Yes, there had been a registered letter for Mr. Jensen on the previous day, and it had been sent from Princetown. Didn't Lowe think it was a very terrible business? And Mr. Sedgwick, too. Such a nice gentleman — very different from Mr. Jensen. Took Pine Cottage because it was quiet and he wanted to write a novel about the moors. And then to suffer a horrible death like that! The aged postmaster shook his bald head. He didn't know what the world was coming to, he really didn't, what with one thing and another. Anyway, he'd be thinking twice now before he ventured out after this. There was no knowing what might happen.

Lowe bought some stamps and, tactfully putting a stop to the old man's flow of small talk, went back to the Rose and Crown. So a registered letter had been delivered at Ridgeway Manor. Young Leyton had spoken the truth. Lowe decided to make inquiries at the post office at Princetown and see if it was possible to obtain a description of the person who had sent it.

The clear, cold frostiness of the morning had given place to a drizzle of rain, and as dusk approached the wind began to rise. It looked as if the night was going to be anything but pleasant.

For the rest of the afternoon until tea-time, Lowe occupied his time writing a long letter to his friend, Inspector Shadgold of Scotland Yard, asking for certain information regarding the past life of Elmer N. Jensen and Sedgwick. Having sent White out to post it, he settled down to hot toasted crumpets and homemade cake with a feeling that he had done all that was possible.

Major Strickland dropped in on his way home to see if they had any further news. He had already heard about the murder of Sedgwick, and was thunderstruck and as completely bewildered as Lowe himself. He couldn't stay very long, but promised to come along to lunch on the following day.

The rain was now pelting down in sheets, and the wind drove it against the window-panes in rattling gusts, howling round the Rose and Crown like a legion of lost souls seeking sanctuary.

Lowe and White had dined, and the latter was yawning over a book and thinking about bed when there came a thunderous knock at the outer door. The bar had been closed for over an hour, and Lowe wondered who it could be who was seeking admission on such a night and at such an hour. He heard the shuffling footsteps of the landlord along the passage and the rattle of bolts as he unfastened the front door. A high-pitched, excited voice reached his ears, there was the sound of hurried feet outside the door, and the next instant it was flung violently open.

John Leyton, hatless and drenched to the skin, stood on the threshold!

'What on earth — ' began the dramatist, rising to his feet, but the secretary's face checked the words that hovered on his tongue. It was as white as paper, and his eyes were drawn and haggard and blazed from their sockets.

'What's the matter, man?' asked Trevor Lowe sharply as Leyton staggered slightly and gripped the back of a chair to steady himself.

'Dorothy!' gasped the secretary, his breath coming in great painful gulps. 'I've run — all the way from — the manor — '

'Miss Jensen!' said Lowe. 'What's the matter with her?'

'I don't know.' Leyton seemed to have the greatest difficulty in speaking at all.

'That's — the terrible part of it.'

'Pull yourself together, Leyton,' cried the dramatist as the other almost broke down, 'and tell me exactly what's happened.'

The secretary sank into a chair and for a second covered his face with his hands. When he raised his head, the wild look had partially subsided.

'Dorothy has disappeared,' he said hopelessly. 'She went out for a walk after tea and hasn't come back since!'

8

Back to the Inn

'But,' protested Lowe, 'there may be several explanations for her absence. She may have called on some friends and they've persuaded her to stay on account of the weather.'

'Dorothy hasn't any friends round here,' replied Leyton. 'Besides, you haven't heard everything. When she hadn't turned up at dinner-time, I went out to see if I could find her. Her favourite walk is along Blackbarrow Coombe and up past the Black Moor Inn, so I went that way. There was no sign of Dorothy until I got to within a hundred yards of the inn, and then I kicked against something that was lying in the road.' He felt in his pocket and took out a sodden bag. 'That's hers,' he said huskily. 'And look — by the clasp!'

Lowe took the bag from Leyton's outstretched hand, and a little thrill of apprehension went through him as he saw the dark red stains on the grey suede. 'Blood!' he murmured softly.

Leyton nodded. 'Yes. Something terrible has happened — I'm sure of it. I thought at first that perhaps Dorothy had fallen down and hurt herself and gone into the Black Moor Inn to recover, but the place was all locked up and in complete darkness. I knocked, but nobody came; and then I went back to Ridgeway, hoping against hope that she would be there. She wasn't, and they'd seen no sign of her. The telephone is still out of order, so I ran all the way here. What's happened to her? What in heaven's name can we do?'

Trevor Lowe gazed at the bag, which he still held in his hand, and the expression on his face was very grave. This was a new and totally unexpected development. Had the same hand that had struck down Jensen and Sedgwick now raised itself against Jensen's daughter? Was Dorothy Jensen the third victim of this unknown killer, and was her body lying cold and lifeless somewhere on the moor under the driving rain and wind? It seemed only too probable, and the dramatist's heart sank for the white-faced figure of the man in the chair.

'There is only one thing to be done,' he said crisply after a slight pause. 'We must go up to the place where you found this bag and see if we can discover any further traces.' He poured out a stiff whisky and handed it to the secretary. 'Drink this,' he said, 'while White and I get our coats on.'

Leyton gulped down the neat spirit, and a tinge of colour crept back into his ashen cheeks. He pushed the wet wisps of hair off his forehead and rose to his feet.

Lowe and White had already struggled into their coats, and the dramatist, making sure that his electric torch was in his pocket, called the landlord. To that astonished man he briefly explained that they had to go out and that they might be late, and arranged for him to wait up for them.

The wind had dropped when they set off on their long journey to the place where Leyton had picked up Dorothy's bag, but the rain still fell with monotonous regularity. When they reached the beginning of Blackbarrow Coombe, they were splashing along through semi-liquid mud. It was this unpleasant state of the road that caused the accident that put White definitely out of the night's happenings. They were swinging along at a sharp pace when he gave a sudden cry and staggered. He would have fallen if Lowe hadn't gripped his arm.

'What's the matter?' asked the dramatist sharply.

'My foot slipped into a rut,' muttered White through his teeth, clenched to hide his agony. 'I think I've twisted my ankle.' He tried to hobble a few yards on the injured foot, but was forced to give up with a groan of anguish. 'It's no good, sir. I'm afraid I'm out of this expedition.'

'You'd better take him back to the Rose and Crown, Leyton,' said the dramatist. 'I can go on and you can join me later. If, as you say, you found the bag about a hundred yards this side of the Black Moor Inn, I can easily find the place by myself, or at any rate near enough for our purpose.'

White protested, but Lowe was insistent, and eventually he and Leyton agreed to obey his orders. They turned back towards the village, White leaning heavily on his companion's arm, and Lowe continued along the coombe alone.

It was a pitch-dark night, and the silence of the countryside was broken only by the soft hiss of the falling rain and the hush-hush of the wind in the branches of the trees. It was bitterly cold. The stinging drops of rain lashed Lowe's face, whipping the blood to the surface and making his cheeks glow. He strode along at a good pace; though, mindful of White's mishap, he was careful where he set his feet, and every now and again flashed his torch ahead. Very soon the road began to take an upward turn, and presently he passed the place where Jensen's body had been discovered.

He was nearing his destination now, and began to walk slower. He was dreading what he might find further along that desolate track on the open moor, for now the road was bounded on either side by long vistas of rain-swept darkness which he knew obscured the rolling moorland.

He had gone about a quarter of a mile further when he decided that he must almost have reached the place where Leyton had found Dorothy's handbag. Switching on his torch, he kept it illuminating the muddy surface at his feet. There were no tracks of any kind, but in this the dramatist was not disappointed. With the rain falling as it was, whatever marks there might have been on that miry slush would soon have been obliterated.

Slowing up so that he barely moved at all, Lowe flashed his light from side to side, but nothing rewarded his search. No crumpled figure lay in the shadows of the night to bring him to a sudden halt.

And then, with nothing but the hiss of the rain and the sighing of the wind around him, a sudden unaccountable feeling stole over him — a sensation that he was being watched. It was distinctly unpleasant, and he tried to shake it off, but it grew. He sensed invisible eyes in the darkness intently watching his every movement. At last the feeling got so strong that he stopped in his search and, standing still, listened carefully.

There was nothing to support that eerie and uncomfortable idea. The wind sighed softly over the open country, and the rain splashed in the puddles at his feet, but no other sound reached his ears. Lowe shrugged his shoulders. He was letting his imagination get the better of him. Of course there was nobody there. Who would be out on the open moor on a night like this? He continued on his way, fanning his light on either side.

A gently sloping hill began to form on the right as he went on, and presently he found himself standing in the little bay that protected the Black Moor Inn from the exposure of the open moorland. He surveyed the unprepossessing building with its ancient sign creaking dismally in the wind. There was no light in any of the windows, and for all the signs of human habitation there were, it might have been empty for years.

Trevor Lowe looked thoughtfully about him. So far he had discovered nothing, and it seemed useless to continue his search in the dark. If — and the thought kept on recurring to him — anything had really happened to Dorothy Jensen, her body must have been taken a considerable distance from the place where she had dropped her handbag. There were any number of places it might be lying, and it was impossible to look thoroughly until daylight — unless it had been taken to the Black Moor Inn.

The idea hit Lowe like a blow on the chin. Supposing Dorothy was somewhere in that gloomy building? She might have been attacked and wounded, but she might not be dead. She might, however, at that moment be dying, and —

He started. This time he had heard something — the stealthy sound of a footfall tiptoeing along the road he had come. He swung round, flashing on his torch, but he was just a second too late.

There came a sudden rush. In the brilliant glare of the torch, he caught a momentary glimpse of a tall figure crouched to spring. The next instant the torch was struck out of his hand.

Something crashed heavily upon his head, and the darkness of the moor rushed into his brain and engulfed his senses.

9

The Cellar of Horror

Trevor Lowe blinked and opened his eyes. He felt dully surprised that his bed was so hard, and wondered vaguely why he was numb with cold, and had such a racking pain in his head. He stretched out his hand into the velvety darkness that surrounded him, and shivered as his groping fingers encountered cold, slimy earth instead of the bedside table as he had expected.

What on earth had happened, and where the deuce was he? This certainly wasn't the comfortable bedroom at the Rose and Crown. Of course it wasn't! He hadn't gone to bed yet. He had gone out to find out what had happened to Dorothy Jensen ...

Suddenly in a flood the whole of the night's events came back to him, including the shadowy figure that had sprung at him out of the darkness while he had been standing outside the Black Moor Inn.

He struggled to a sitting posture. The pain in his head made him wince, but presently it got a little better. Who had struck him, and where had he been taken?

He felt in his pockets, but the torch was no longer there. Either it had been taken from him, or he had lost it when that shape had flung itself on him in the darkness. He remembered the torch being struck from his hand.

Lowe thought for a second, and then began groping in his waistcoat pockets. He usually carried a small gold petrol lighter. Unless that, too, had been taken away, it would provide him with enough light to see his surroundings. It was there, and, stumbling to his feet, he pressed the catch. In the dull glimmer of flame that resulted he gazed around him. —

He was in a small, low-roofed cellar apparently hollowed out of the earth itself, for the walls and floor were composed of moist mould, and slimy with the percolated moisture of ages. His shoes splashed in an inch of foul water, and the air was so close and fetid that the flame of the lighter only burned dimly. Hundreds of great black slugs clung to the earthen walls, hanging perpendicularly like great black fingers.

Trevor Lowe shivered. It was a cellar of horror, a nauseating place, the only dry spot a flight of wooden steps leading up to a pair of cellar flaps; and these were soggy and rotting like decayed seaweed. He looked down at himself. He was covered from head to foot in green, slimy mud! To what horrible place had he been taken?

The pain in his head was making him feel sick and giddy, and he sat for a second or two on the sludgy steps to think things out. He discovered after a search that he had still got his cigarette-case, and he lit a cigarette and smoked steadily into the black silence, the glowing ash lighting up his face redly as he drew in each lungful of smoke. By the time the cigarette had been consumed, he felt better. Rising, he snapped on his lighter, and, ascending the steps, began an examination of the cellar flaps, which apparently formed the entrance and exit to this mud-box into which he had been thrust.

Lowe began to form plans for getting out. The cellar flaps fitted into a six-inch surround of cement, which in its turn was embedded in solid earth, and a test of the heavy oak revealed the fact that the flaps at any rate were immovable. The roof of the cellar, as near as he could judge by the covering of the hatch side, was a little over eighteen inches thick, and there seemed to be a weak patch near the hinge side of the flaps. Some of the earth forming the roof had crumbled away at this point.

Lowe habitually carried a large clasp-knife in his hip pocket, and he slipped his hand under his overcoat with a silent prayer that it hadn't been taken away. It was there, and, opening the blade, he mounted the steps as high as he could get, leaning with one hand against the covering and digging away at the loose earth with the other. He had to work in the dark, but every now and again he flashed on the lighter and inspected his progress. His headway was fairly rapid, as no sooner was a piece of moist earth dislodged than it fell, it being easier to dig a hole from below than from above.

Soon the task became no more than the continuous circling of the knife in the hole that he had already made. A gentle splutter of earth fell softly into the water below. At first it kicked up a dreadful noise in the silence; and once, when a nest of stones fell, he held his breath and listened for long seconds, for it seemed impossible that the din was not audible above.

Presently the falling earth rose above the level of the water, and after that his operations went forward in almost complete silence. The mound of earth rose as the size of the hole grew, and Lowe began to feel the heat of his exertions. He took off his coat and slung it on the wet steps, and also took the opportunity of the pause in his work to shorten the wick in the lighter. There couldn't be much more petrol in it, and he had to economize.

He continued his excavations, and suddenly came upon the stumbling-block. The roof evidently formed the floor of some room above, for he found that the earth had been reinforced with lines of wooden rafters. He was making a hole about eighteen inches in diameter, and he scraped away until he had laid the rafters bare. Then began a slow and painful hacking through the timber. The wood, however, buried in damp earth for God knew how long, was not the tough, resilient stuff it had been when first the builders had sunk it there. Age had sapped its fibres and damp had decayed its strength, though it was still far from rotten.

Lowe's wrists tingled through and through; his fingers had gone dead from gripping the slim knife-handle, and his arms throbbed with the effort of holding them continuously above his head, but he stuck gamely to his task. At the end of an hour he took a rest, smoking another cigarette. One section of the timber had fallen, and another was half hacked through. When they were down, there were still two more to be dislodged. He lay back on his coat and let his arms hang limp and lifeless.

After that he worked in spells — ten minutes at the roof and five to rest his aching arms. The third rafter fell at his fifth spell; he cheated ten minutes of bone-aching labour by getting his fingers over the joist and swinging on it. His weight snapped it and he fell into the mud and water with a crash. But it was a lesson learnt, and in half an hour the last of the rafters had been dislodged.

The rest of the business was almost pleasant after the racking labour of chewing through the wood with his knife-blade. The blade had broken, but once the timbers were down that didn't matter much. With only soft earth to penetrate, it added, if anything, to the efficacy of the instrument.

And now there arose the problem as to whether it was safe to continue. Only a thin crust separated him from whatever lay above, and Lowe had no particular wish to emerge from his prison into the arms, as it were, of the man who had put him there.

He looked at his watch, flicking on his lighter to see the hands. The wick flamed up brightly for a second, bobbed irritatingly once or twice, and fluttered out, the petrol exhausted. The wick end still smouldered pungently, and Lowe utilized the last spark to light a final cigarette.

It was barely half-past twelve. He hadn't the least idea where he would emerge, though he gave a shrewd guess that it was somewhere in the vicinity of the Black Moor Inn, if not actually inside the inn itself. The question was, would there be anybody about?

He let an hour slip by and then decided to risk it, not so much because it was now safe, but because the chill clamminess of the place was getting into his bones. There was a wet coldness in the air that was numbing. It seemed to creep and crawl through him, blotting out all warmth and slowly but surely sapping at his own bodily heat. Another two hours of that, he knew, would see him a shivering mass of quivering flesh too cold and numb to work; too dulled with the cold even to make a fight for it when the time came.

He re-ascended the steps and began pounding away at the hole again with renewed energy. A few seconds later the stub of his knife struck something hard and solid. He guessed it was either a stone slab or concrete, and his heart sank. Carefully he picked away, clearing the whole of the mud from this fresh obstruction. Feeling around in the darkness, his fingers encountered the chinks and crevices of stone setts. He gave a sigh of relief. He was not to be cheated of his freedom at the last moment.

And then, suddenly and without warning, the whole lot collapsed down the hole, falling with a tremendous clatter into the cellar beneath and missing Lowe's head by a couple of inches as he jerked himself hurriedly back from the gaping aperture!

10

What Lowe Overheard

Trevor Lowe waited with his nerves tensed. 'Now for it!' he muttered, and listened. It seemed impossible that that appalling crash could have passed unnoticed if there had been any human being within hearing.

He waited minute after minute, his nerves tingling like taut piano wires, but nothing happened. There was no sound. He was on the point of moving when from somewhere overhead he heard a soft rustling, and then a long-drawn, painful sigh. It seemed to come from just above the gaping hole he had excavated. There was the faintest afterglow of light percolating down through that hole, no more than the reflected glimmer in one dark room of a coal fire burning in another. It was not even strong enough to make the sides of the hole visible to him. Lowe wondered what it was.

The silence of the grave seemed to

have settled over the place, and, gaining courage from the entire absence of any further sounds, Lowe leaned forward and cautiously tried to peer up the opening. But it was like looking up the walls of the night. Except for that vaguely reflected suggestion of light, the place was as dark as the tomb. There was no direct filtration of light rays, and the dramatist became more and more puzzled. There was nothing overhead that he could see, and yet there was certainly a light coming from somewhere.

He placed his hands on the edges of the hole, and was testing them with a view to pulling himself up, when a fresh sound came from above — the harsh grating of a key in a lock, followed by the sound of footfalls over his head! Removing his hands, he stood stock-still, listening. Unless a miracle happened, the newcomer would discover the hole, and — what then?

Lowe tensed his muscles, waiting for the sharp exclamation that would denote the person above had seen it. But that exclamation didn't come. Instead he heard a muffled voice say huskily: 'Has she recovered?'

There was a grunt, and another footstep

became audible: a shuffling, slouching step. Then a thick, husky voice replied in a guttural whisper: 'I don't know — better see for yerself, ain't yer?'

'You've been at the drink again, my friend,' said the first speaker in that curiously muffled tone. 'Can't you keep off it until we've finished this job?'

'I don't like the job,' grumbled the other. 'You forced me inter it, and I've been scared stiff ever since Jensen was croaked, expecting the perlice at any moment.'

'Well, they wouldn't have found anything if they'd come,' answered his companion. 'The whole thing would have passed for an accident, as I intended, if that clever Trevor Lowe hadn't happened to have been in the neighbourhood. That was bad luck.'

'An' I s'pose it was more bad luck that sent 'im snooping round 'ere after you'd collared the woman,' sneered the thick, drunken voice unsteadily.

Lowe heard a smothered chuckle. 'No, that was good luck, Box,' was the reply. 'The best of luck, because now he's safe and out of the way, and not likely to trouble anybody anymore.'

'That's all very well,' argued Box, 'but what about 'is friends? They'll be buzzin' round 'ere like flies round a jam-pot when they finds he's missin'.'

'But I keep on telling you, you fool,' snarled the other angrily, 'that they can't find anything. As soon as I've got the information I want from the woman, I'll attend to her and Lowe as well, and then when they're found somewhere out on the moor there'll be nothing to connect you or me or the Black Moor Inn with their deaths.'

So, thought Lowe, he was at the Black Moor Inn, and it was from the Black Moor Inn that Jensen had been brought and laid under that pile of gravel. The proprietor, Box, was the owner of the thick, drunken voice. Who was the other man? There was something vaguely familiar about his voice, but Lowe couldn't remember what it was. He was obviously the instigator of the business, Box merely an unwilling tool.

Apparently, from this conversation, Dorothy Jensen was also in the building. The most mysterious thing of all was why they hadn't discovered the hole. Perhaps they were in another room adjoining the one the hole opened into, and their voices carried through an open door. Lowe stopped his ruminations and listened again as Box began speaking.

'The gal's recovered,' he growled. 'For God's sake, find out whatever it is yer want ter know and get finished 'ere.'

'You seem mighty anxious to get rid of me,' chuckled the other.

'I am,' declared the innkeeper fervently. 'Awl the time yer 'ere I'm in danger.'

'Be useful for a change and remove her gag,' was the reply, and Lowe heard shuffling footsteps come nearer. There was no mistake now. They were almost on the edge of the hole — they must see it.

But they did not. To the dramatist's increasing mystification, the footsteps stopped, and there followed a creaking sound and then a long sigh.

'What — what am I doing here?' came a husky whisper. 'I — oh — !' The broken sentence ended in a little strangled scream. The voice that had spoken was that of Dorothy Jensen.

'You have nothing to fear — at present,' said the man who was with Box, 'if you will give me the information I want.'

Trevor Lowe smiled grimly. That assurance of safety didn't coincide with what those two above had been planning before Dorothy had recovered consciousness.

'Information?' Her voice was stronger and steadier. 'What information can I give you? Who are you?'

She didn't lack courage, thought the dramatist. After that first cry she had quickly recovered herself.

'Never mind who I am,' said the other impatiently. 'That's no concern of yours. What I want to know is, what did your father do with the diamonds?'

'Diamonds? What diamonds?' asked Dorothy, and her tone was rather puzzled.

'It's no good pretending you didn't know anything about them,' snarled her questioner. 'Your father had three hundred of them. Uncut diamonds, looking like grey-green pebbles.'

'I know nothing about them. If my father ever had them, he never told me anything about it.'

There was a momentary pause, and in the silence Lowe heard again the faint creaking sound. 'It's no use lying,' went on the muffled voice. 'You'll stay here until you do tell me.'

'How can I tell you what I know nothing about? And you can't keep me here bound to this bed forever.'

So that was the explanation of the creaking noise, thought Lowe. They had bound her to some sort of truckle bed, and it was the rasping of the thin iron slats that he had heard.

'I don't intend to keep you there forever.' The harsh voice was speaking again. 'I shall give you a few hours to make up your mind and tell me where those diamonds are hidden, or you'll go the same way as your father went.'

Dorothy gave a little exclamation — the choked cry of one who was trying desperately to retain her courage. 'You mean — you intend to kill me?' she murmured.

'I mean just that,' snarled the other. 'So you'd better hurry up and be sensible. I shall come back in an hour and see if you've changed your mind.'

There was a shuffling of footsteps, and the thud of a closing door — then silence broken by a smothered sob. Trevor Lowe listened, but there was no other sound from above. He decided that it was time he discovered what exactly lay beyond the hole, and solve the incredible mystery of the fact that the men above had stood practically on the brink of that aperture in the floor without seeing it.

He leaned over from the steps, gripped the edge of the hole with his lean fingers, and hauled himself up. With a tremendous effort of strength, he got his head up above the level of the aperture, his feet and legs swinging out in space over the floor below.

For a moment he rested and looked about. But nothing but that vague darkness, relieved by the touch of reflected light, met his eyes. Presently he heaved himself up, got an arm clear, and levered up the rest of his body over the hole. And in doing so, his head came into violent contact with an unseen object above — such a heavy blow that it nearly knocked him bodily back again through the hole into the cellar beneath!

11

The Fight at the Inn

It took Lowe a few seconds to recover from that blow on the head, and two further minutes of precarious slipping and scrambling before he finally got out of the hole onto cold, solid ground. Lying flat on his chest, he waited to get his breath back, and then tried to discover where he was.

Down on the floor level was a thin, horizontal chink of stronger light. He put out his hand and touched something that swayed about and made the crack of light wobble. It was a fabric of some sort, a draping that hung down to within half an inch of the floor. He felt carefully about him. Overhead was something hard and metallic. He explored along further with his fingers and found that there was a queer roofing of metal springs two feet above his head. In a flash he knew where he was. That queer roofing was the underside of the bed on which Dorothy lay, and the fabric was the draping at the sides.

He had excavated the hole by sheer chance right under the bed. It accounted for the obscurity of the light, and for the strange fact that neither of the men had seen the hole. It was the springs against which he had cannoned his head when he pulled himself up.

Lowe crawled out from under the bed and looked about him. He was in a low, very dirty cellar, the corners of which were stacked with barrels and empty bottles — the storage cellar evidently for the inn. The walls were of rough brickwork, and the low ceiling was formed by the rafters of the floor above. An oil lamp stood on an upturned grate at the side of a truckle iron bedstead. It was covered with a filthy blanket that trailed on the floor all round, and on this lay Dorothy Jensen, her wrists and ankles bound to the head and bottom rails of the bed.

Her face was deathly white, and across her forehead was a long scratch, from which the blood had oozed and dried on her cheek. Her eyes were wide and staring as she gazed with horror at the dramatist, and there was a reason for her look, for no one would have recognized Lowe in the mud-plastered, slime-covered object that emerged from under the bed.

He rose to his feet and laid a finger to his lips. 'Don't make a sound, Miss Jensen,' he whispered hurriedly as she opened her mouth. 'It's me, Trevor Lowe.'

The horror in her eyes changed to an expression of almost ludicrous surprise. 'Mr. Lowe?' she breathed. 'But — where did you come from? How did you get here?'

'There's no time for explanations now. We need to get out of here.'

He went over to the door and cautiously tried it. It was made of stout oak, and immovable. A quick examination showed the impossibility of shifting that barrier. Lowe made a hurried search of the cellar to see if there was any other means of egress, but discovered none. In one corner were the flaps, secured by a heavy oak bar that led into the mud-hole from which he had escaped, but that was all. It seemed at first glance that he had only got out of the frying pan into the fire.

And then an idea struck him. The man with the muffled voice had said he would come back in an hour. He had as yet no inkling that the dramatist had got out of the mud prison below. If Lowe concealed himself beneath the bed, a possible chance of tackling and overpowering the fellow might present itself. It was the only course of action available, so far as Lowe could see, and in a few brief sentences he suggested it to Dorothy. 'In the meanwhile,' he said, 'I'll loosen these cords at your wrists and ankles so that they'll look the same, but if necessary you can get free.'

He set about the task, and while he was busy at the knots, Dorothy gave him a brief account of how she had been set upon in the dark. She had been in the habit for some time of taking a walk after tea, but was usually accompanied by Leyton. Today, however, she had wanted to be alone, and, putting on a mackintosh, had set off in the drizzle up the coombe. She had seen nobody, which hadn't surprised her, for few people came along that way, since it led nowhere except to the open moor and the inn, and the villagers preferred the nearer and more comfortable hospitality of the Rose and Crown.

Almost at the end of Blackbarrow Coombe, however, she had heard somebody walking along ahead of her. The night was too dark for her to see who it was, but thinking it was possibly some labourer returning to his cottage after his day's work, she had taken very little notice.

At the point where the coombe frayed out into the open moorland path, she had overtaken a tall, muffled figure striding along in the same direction as she was going. She had passed within a yard of the man, scarcely giving him a glance, and continued on her way. It had been her intention to walk as far as the Black Moor Inn and then turn back and go home; but when she had got to about a hundred yards away from the inn, she had heard running footsteps behind her. Alarmed, she had half-turned; but before she could cry out or even see what was happening, she had been seized roughly by the throat, something had crashed down on her forehead, and she had lost consciousness.

After that she had a dim recollection of being carried into some building, and of having some bitter-tasting stuff forced down her throat. It had made her feel sick, and then everything had gone black. She remembered nothing more until she had awakened to find herself lying on the bed, bound as Lowe had found her; and with two men, one of whom she recognized as Box the innkeeper, bending over her.

'What about the other man?' asked Trevor Lowe as she paused in her whispered recital.

'I don't know who he was,' she answered. 'I didn't see his face. He wore some sort of a black handkerchief tied round his nose, mouth and chin. I only saw his eyes beneath the brim of his hat.'

The dramatist loosened the last knot and straightened. 'What about those diamonds he was questioning you about? Do you know anything concerning them?'

'Nothing at all. I've never heard my father mention them. If he ever had them, he kept the fact to himself.'

There were several things Lowe would have liked to ask her, but it was dangerous just at that moment to risk even the low conversation they had been having. In the complete silence of the old inn, sound travelled; and if the men above got the slightest inkling that Lowe had succeeded in breaking out of his mud prison, then his plan, and with it all chance of escape, would be futile. There would be plenty of time for questions later when they were free — if they were lucky enough to get free.

At least he had learned one thing — Box was in the business up to his neck, and it shouldn't prove a difficult matter to make him talk once he was arrested and under lock and key. At the moment there was nothing to do but await the return of the man with the muffled voice and trust to luck.

The time passed slowly, but presently Lowe heard the sound of a movement above. Somebody was walking across the floor, the supports of which formed the ceiling to the cellar. A door opened, and footsteps descended a flight of stairs. With a sign to Dorothy, Lowe dropped onto his chest and wriggled his way under the bed. Arranging the overhanging blanket so that he could see the door, he lay and watched expectantly.

The footsteps came along outside and stopped. There was the clanking noise of bolts being drawn back, and then the heavy door opened. The tall figure of a man in a long coat that fell almost to his heels entered. The dramatist saw that he wore a slouch hat drawn low over his eyes, and that the bottom half of his face was concealed beneath a piece of black material. He stood for a moment on the threshold, and then, closing the door behind him, approached the bed. Box evidently had remained behind this time somewhere upstairs, probably sampling some more of his own beer.

All the better, thought Lowe. *If I can only manage somehow to secure this fellow, I can take the other by surprise. Overpowering him in his half-fuddled state ought to be easy.*

The masked man came nearer to the bed and looked down at Dorothy. 'Well,' he demanded harshly, 'have you changed your mind?'

There was an almost imperceptible pause before she replied. 'There is nothing to change,' she said at length. 'I've already told you, I know nothing about what you asked me.'

'Still obstinate, eh?' he retorted menacingly. 'Well, I warn you, my patience is exhausted. For the last time, tell me where Jensen put those diamonds!'

'How can I when I don't know? I've never —' She broke off with a little cry as, giving a snarl of rage, the man sprang forward.

'I'll make you speak if I have to choke the life out of you!' he hissed thickly.

Trevor Lowe thought it was time he acted. Within a foot of him were the man's ankles, and suddenly shooting out his hands, the dramatist gripped them and jerked them forward with all his strength. He heard a muffled howl of surprise from above, and then the man by the bed overbalanced and fell backwards with a crash on the stone floor.

Lowe hauled himself swiftly from his hiding place, and had half-risen to his feet when the man sprang up and hurled himself bodily on him. They went down together, rolling over and over, each clawing frantically for a hold. The masked man possessed prodigious strength, but Lowe's knowledge of wrestling did a lot to outweigh it. He was certainly getting the advantage, when they cannoned into the crate and sent it flying together with the lamp, which fell with a thud on the dramatist's head, rebounded and crashed to pieces on the floor. The sudden darkness and the momentary shock of the blow caused Lowe to release his hold. His opponent took instant advantage and tore himself free. And at that precise moment, there came a thunderous knocking from somewhere above.

With a muttered imprecation, the masked man scrambled to his feet, eluded Trevor Lowe's wild effort to stop him, and made a dash for the door. Lowe was up by this time, but the man banged the door in his face as he reached it, and the dramatist heard his footsteps go scurrying up the stairs.

As Lowe wrenched open the door and followed, the knocking was repeated. A thick, blurred voice that he recognized as Box's was muttering something from the top of a flight of steps that ran upwards from the narrow passage outside the cellar door. He heard a snarled reply, followed by a little choking, cough-like sound and a heavy thud — then silence.

Rushing up the wooden steps, which led to a trap in the floor above, Lowe leaped through the square aperture and found himself in the tap-room. A dirty white gas globe cast a sickly light over the place, and a glance served to show that it was empty. A half-open door leading into darkness beyond was opposite the filthy bar, and Lowe made for this exit.

As he crossed the threshold, he almost stumbled over something that was lying huddled up on the floor. Stooping, he felt about and touched — a human face! With a little suppressed shudder, the dramatist pulled the door wide open so that the light from the tap-room flooded the passageway beyond.

A man lay still and motionless just outside the door, his staring eyes fixed in a rigid glare at the shadow-shrouded ceiling. It was Box, and he was dead!

12

Dorothy Jensen Speaks

Trevor Lowe was still gazing down at the dead innkeeper with a feeling of mingled amazement and horror when again came that thunderous knocking, this time louder than before. Someone was battering at the front door, and after a momentary hesitation the dramatist felt his way along the dark passage and fumbled at the bolts and chain. While he was getting the door open, he heard a voice that he recognized as Leyton's whisper: 'Here's someone coming at last!' Opening the door, he made out two figures standing on the threshold, dim and shadowy in the darkness.

'Have you — ' began the gruff voice of Inspector Rooper, and then Lowe interrupted him.

'Come in, both of you,' said the dramatist.

Leyton gave a little gasp of astonishment.

'Lowe!' he exclaimed. 'Good God, man, what are you doing here? Have you found Dorothy? Where did you — '

'I'll tell you all about it in a moment,' broke in Lowe, checking the stream of questions. 'Miss Jensen is here and quite safe.'

The secretary uttered a sigh of relief and stepped across the threshold, followed by the inspector.

'I wondered what the deuce had become of you,' said Lowe.

'I came up here after taking White back to the Rose and Crown, but I couldn't see a sign of anybody,' answered Leyton. 'I thought perhaps you'd found Dorothy and gone over to Ridgeway Manor, so I went back there, but there was no news at all. From there I went to the Rose and Crown, but you hadn't gone back there, either. I admit I was getting a bit anxious, and I thought I'd rake out Inspector Rooper. He wasn't at the station, but they gave me his address, and I went and hunted him out of bed and told him what had happened.'

'When we got to the place where Mr. Leyton had found the bag,' interposed

Rooper, 'and there was still no trace of you, Mr. Lowe, I thought we'd knock up Box and see if he'd seen or heard anything.'

'It's very lucky you're here, Inspector,' said the dramatist, 'though I'm afraid Box won't be able to tell us much. He'll neither see nor hear anything again.'

'What do you mean?' exclaimed the startled Rooper.

'I mean,' answered Trevor Lowe grimly, 'that Box is dead! Come here.' He led the way along the dark passage and pointed down silently at the crumpled form that lay in the dim fan of light from the tap-room.

'Good God!' muttered the inspector. 'How did this happen, Mr. Lowe? Who killed him?'

'The same man who killed Jensen and Sedgwick,' said Lowe. 'The same man who waylaid Miss Jensen and brought her here. I don't know who he is, but Box did. That's why he died. Our unknown killer made sure before he escaped that the innkeeper wouldn't have a chance of squealing.'

He gave a short, succinct account of what had happened from the time he had been attacked outside the Black Moor Inn, and the inspector listened, his mouth half-open and an expression of almost ludicrous incredulity on his weather-beaten face.

'Well,' he exclaimed at length when the dramatist had finished, 'there ain't no lack of incidents in this business, is there, sir? I'd never 'ave believed such things could 'ave 'appened round Stoneford.'

'Is Dorothy still in this cellar place?' asked young Leyton.

Lowe nodded. 'That's where I left her.'

'I'll go and see if she's all right,' muttered the secretary, and hurried away.

When they were alone Lowe, and the inspector made a closer examination of the body. A pool of crimson had oozed from underneath since the dramatist had looked at it before. Gently turning the still form over, Lowe pointed to the bone handle of a knife that protruded from between the shoulder-blades.

'Stabbed from behind,' he said quietly. 'Box must have turned to leave the tap-room when the murderer struck him.'

The inspector scratched his head. 'The whole thing's getting me down,' he declared. 'It seems to me that there must be an 'omicidal maniac loose around 'ere.'

'The man who was trying to make Miss Jensen tell him where her father had hidden those diamonds was no homicidal maniac,' said Trevor Lowe decisively. 'He was as sane as you or me. Besides, the motive for killing Box is clear enough. He heard you knocking at the door, and before he made his escape he took precautions to ensure his own safety. Box knew him, and undoubtedly if he'd been arrested and questioned, would have told all he knew to try and save his own skin. The unknown killed him to make certain of his silence.'

'I wonder what can be at the bottom of it all?' muttered Rooper, screwing up his eyes in perplexity.

'I think those uncut diamonds have got a lot to do with it, though not by any means all, because they don't explain the reason for the murder of Sedgwick.'

'The thing that beats me is where this murderer can be hiding. He must be living somewhere in the neighbourhood.'

'Or at Princetown,' added the dramatist. 'Don't forget that the registered letter Jensen received on the day of his death, and which apparently was the cause of his going out on that stormy night, was posted in Princetown.'

Before the inspector could make any further remark, young Leyton reappeared with Dorothy. The combined effects of the drug and her terrifying experience of the night had taken their toll of her, and she looked haggard and ill. Her face was a grey-white in contrast to the usual freshness of her complexion, and beneath her eyes were crescent-shaped smudges of purple. In spite of her obvious physical unfitness, however, her spirit remained unbroken, for she steadfastly refused all Leyton's suggestions that he should take her home.

'Presently,' she said firmly. 'I'm quite all right except for a headache, and I'd much rather wait here until you've all finished.'

The secretary, with a shrug of his shoulders, gave up all attempts at further persuasion. Settling Dorothy in a chair by the tap-room fireplace, he stirred the dying embers in the grate to a blaze. He found a bottle of brandy behind the bar and, opening it, poured out a stiff drink and insisted that Dorothy have some. After a little hesitation she complied.

The neat spirit took some of the grey tinge from her cheeks and brought a little of the old sparkle back to her eyes.

Noticing that Inspector Rooper was eyeing the bottle a trifle wistfully, Lowe suggested that a drink all round wouldn't do them any harm. When Leyton had attended to this and Rooper had drained his, smacking his lips appreciatively, he and the inspector went off on a search of the inn. However, they found nothing whatever that shed the smallest ray of light on the problem, or suggested the identity of the masked man.

The whole place was indescribably dirty. Box appeared to have lived alone and attended to his own wants, which, from the number of empty bottles in his bedroom, seemed to have been mostly of a liquid nature. Having been over the entire building from cellar to attic and found nothing, the secretary and the inspector returned to the tap-room. Leyton made up the fire from a bucket of coal that stood by the hearth, and its cheerful blaze dispelled some of the gloom, though it couldn't remove the horror of that silent figure in the passage.

Rooper volunteered to go back to Stoneford and fetch an ambulance and Dr. Macaulay. After he had gone out into the now-thinning drizzle, Lowe lighted a cigarette; and, having closed the door to shut out the visible signs of the tragedy that had taken place there, he drew up a chair to the fire. 'Do you feel strong and well enough to answer a few questions, Miss Jensen?' he asked after he had smoked for a few moments in silence.

She nodded. 'If you think I can help you in any way,' she replied; 'though I really know nothing more than I've already told you.'

'That's hardly an accurate statement, is it?' murmured the dramatist.

She shot him a quick sidelong glance. 'What do you mean?'

'I mean you haven't told me everything,' said Trevor Lowe, blowing a cloud of smoke from his lips and watching it rise and slowly disperse. 'For instance, you haven't told me why you and Mr. Leyton took such pains to search your father's papers before Inspector Rooper and I arrived at Ridgeway, or the reason which induced you to make that search.'

Dorothy had been staring into the roaring fire. Now she turned her head and looked at Lowe steadily. Before she could say anything, however, young Leyton broke in angrily.

'What the devil do you mean, Lowe?' he demanded. 'Are you accusing Miss Jensen and me of lying?'

'No; I am merely suggesting that you've been holding something back,' said the dramatist quietly. 'And I should like to know what it is.'

There was a long silence. Dorothy's gaze had returned to the fire; but presently, as though she had made up her mind, she looked round. 'You're quite right, Mr. Lowe,' she said. 'I — we — have been holding something back, but it can have no bearing on my — my father's death.'

'I should rather like to be the judge of that,' answered Trevor Lowe.

'I'd rather not say anything about it. I give you my word that it's purely a personal matter.'

'Then it can do no harm if you tell me,' persisted the dramatist. 'If it has no bearing on the case, then I, in my turn, will give my word that it will go no further than this room.'

Again there was a long silence, and then: 'Very well, Mr. Lowe. It's just this. Everyone has been under the impression that I was Elmer N. Jensen's daughter. I was not. Who my parents were, I don't know, but the man who was supposed to be my father bore no relation to me whatever.'

13

The Next to Die

Trevor Lowe got back to the Rose and Crown shortly after four, feeling dead tired, but with his mind so occupied that he felt it would be a long time before sleep came to him.

White had gone to bed after bandaging his sprained ankle, but was still awake. The dramatist, after a bath to rid himself of the mud and slime he had collected in the noisome cellar of the Black Moor Inn, arrayed himself in pyjamas and dressing gown, and, sitting on his secretary's bed, smoked a pipe and acquainted White with the latest developments.

'So you see,' he concluded, 'at least one little mystery is cleared up. Jensen, in a fit of temper one day, informed Dorothy that she wasn't his daughter at all. He refused to tell her, however, who her real father was. So, when it was found that he was missing that morning, she and Leyton, whom she had taken into her confidence, took the opportunity to search the study in the hope they would find something that would establish her identity.'

'I don't see why they wanted to keep it secret, though,' said White. 'Why didn't she want to tell you?'

'For two reasons, both equally good ones,' answered his employer. 'First, because she didn't want any publicity about the fact that she wasn't Jensen's daughter; and second, because so far as she could tell, he died without leaving a will. Now Jensen was a rich man — how rich, we shan't know until his solicitor goes through his affairs. Leyton has been in touch with him, and he's coming down tomorrow — or, rather, today.

'You see, the position so far as Dorothy is concerned is this. If Jensen hasn't left a will, his estate would — in the ordinary course of events, if she is still counted as his daughter — go to her as next of kin. If, however, the point was raised that she was no relation whatever, it's doubtful if she would get anything. We can scarcely blame her for wishing to keep the fact to herself.'

'No, I suppose not,' agreed White. 'Anyway, it doesn't seem to have much bearing on the mystery, so it makes no difference.'

Trevor Lowe knocked the ashes out of his pipe. 'That's rather a sweeping statement to make,' he said. 'It may possibly have a tremendous bearing on the mystery.'

'How?'

'Well, our present difficulty is the absence of motive in these crimes. With the exception of Box, we don't know why they've taken place. The diamonds may have been the reason for Jensen's death, but we don't know, and therefore we have to look for every possible motive — a motive also that embraces Sedgwick.

'Now, since Dorothy turns out to be not Miss Jensen at all, but somebody else, she must have had parents. Who these parents are, we don't know, but it's practically a certainty that Jensen wasn't her father. Who *were* her parents, and are they still alive? And why did Jensen adopt the child? It seems from all accounts of his character that it was hardly from an altruistic motive; therefore there's a distinct possibility that this adoption of an unknown child whom he passed off as his daughter may provide the reason for his death.'

'But what about the uncut diamonds?' objected White. 'How do they come into it?'

'They may, for all we know, be stolen property. Nobody except Sedgwick appears to have known of their existence — nobody, that is, apart from our unknown murderer. Supposing, for instance, that the diamonds belonged to Dorothy's real parents, and Jensen had stolen the stones; that would provide a very good motive for his murder.'

'But it wouldn't explain why he should have adopted the child.'

'No, it wouldn't. Perhaps when we get the information I've sent for regarding his past, we shall get some clue to that. One thing I'm convinced of is that Jensen and Sedgwick were old acquaintances — that their lives were so strongly linked together that the same motive for Jensen's death applies to the murder of Sedgwick. However ... ' He rose with a yawn and stretched himself. ' ... I'm not going to theorize any more now. I'm going to bed.

Good night!'

'Good *morning*,' retorted his secretary with a grin. 'Sleep well.'

But Lowe did not sleep well. His mind was full of a chaotic whirl of theory, conjecture and possibilities as he got into bed. Although, physically tired as he was, he fell into an uneasy slumber almost before his head had lain long enough on the pillow to warm its coldness, he was troubled with vague, disconnected dreams in which a huge shadowy figure with an upraised sword stalked about an impossible countryside, slaying incredible people who possessed grey-green stones for faces.

Soon it seemed the figure became much nearer. As it approached, it grew bigger and bigger, and with its nearness there came upon the dramatist a sensation of suffocation. For a second or so Lowe's mind was wandering in the mists of sleep. Then all of a sudden he came back to full consciousness and reality.

It was to find a masked man bending over him. In the figure's hand was a long tube, at the end of which was a padded mouthpiece from which came a gush of gas. Lowe tried to rise, tried to ward off the choking fumes. But he had wakened too late! His feeble struggles ceased, and his head fell back on the pillow. His senses had gone, and he lay like one dead as the masked figure swiftly climbed out of the window and vanished into the night.

An interminable time afterwards, as it appeared, Lowe became aware of a stifling oppression underlaid by a feeling of unutterable nausea. The awareness widened to an instinctive knowledge of the proximity of some living thing.

'Hello!' said an immensely remote voice. 'Thank God yer still alive, sir!'

A narrow beam of light cut across the grey darkness of the room and rested on Lowe's face. *Extraordinary*, he thought dully. *An electric torch.* And the person who had spoken was the combined boots-and pot-man at the Rose and Crown. What on earth was the boots doing in his room?

Lowe decided that he would demand an answer. He raised himself by a mighty effort on one elbow to do it and sank back again, sickly dizzy. He was conscious now of a noxious heaviness in the air he was breathing. All his senses revolted at it. He made another strenuous effort to sit up, to get out of bed, to get out of that poisonous atmosphere.

And then, to the exclusion of all other considerations, he was suddenly and violently sick. The boots-man, muttering all the time, ministered to his needs efficiently, if somewhat urgently, by the light of the torch.

Presently Lowe began to feel better, and saw by the wavering illumination what appeared to him at first to be a coil of red rope lying on the pillow beside him. Gradually he became aware that it was the end of a piece of red rubber tubing that trailed over the brass rail of his bed into the dimness behind him. It was some little time before the phenomenon began to arouse active interest in his numbed brain.

He reached out a shaking hand and caught the red coil. Yes, it was rubber tubing — with a wide mouthpiece. Why rubber tubing on his bed, and how had it got there? He made a great effort to think clearly, and the memory came back to him in a flash. But he was in no mind to confide in the boots-man.

'Look here!' he demanded weakly. 'What are you doing in my room?'

The man replied with a question. 'Are you better now, sir? Lor', yer did give me a turn! I smelt the gas when I came round collecting the boots. It's lucky yer left yer door unlocked. I've opened the windows now, sir; but when I first found yer — phew! — the room was full of gas.' He stopped, and then asked curiously and not without a tinge of suspicion in his voice: 'What was yer a-tryin' ter do, sir?'

Before the dramatist could answer, a recurrence of the deadly nausea gripped him and rendered all speech impossible. Together with the cold air that was streaming in through the open windows, however, it had the effect of clearing his brain and making him feel a little more like himself. He listened while the boots-man recounted his story. He had been on his morning's round when he had smelt gas. He had traced it to Lowe's room and found the door unlocked, and gas streaming from the end of the rubber tubing, which had been attached to the bracket.

The dramatist asked him to make some

strong tea, gave him a ten-shilling note, and suggested that he should keep his mouth shut. Very reluctantly the man agreed to this, though it was obvious that he was under the impression that Lowe had made a determined attempt to commit suicide. He departed, and returned presently with a cup of strong tea, which the dramatist gulped down gratefully. He was still feeling horribly weak and ill, but eventually managed to sleep.

When he awoke, it was broad daylight and his head ached furiously. His first waking thought was of the attempt that had been made on his life during the night. Whose hand had fixed that rubber tubing to the bracket and turned on the gas? Who was the figure he had seen bending over him?

It didn't require a great effort of brain-power to answer that question. Who else but the mysterious killer who had murdered Jensen, Sedgwick and Box?

So the unknown had turned his attention to him, had he? reflected the dramatist grimly. Well, that meant that he was afraid, and there was no better way of catching a criminal than by getting him in a panic. In his efforts to cover his tracks, he usually made the one false move that eventually put him in the dock.

Trevor Lowe hoped that this would prove no exception to the rule. If he had to spend the rest of his life looking for him, he was determined to find the man who had turned on that gas-tap.

14

The Yard Takes a Hand

As Trevor Lowe rose and proceeded rather dizzily with his toilet, he began to wonder just how the attempt on his life had been carried out. While he lathered his face preparatory to shaving, he went over to one of the two windows and looked out, continuing to use the shaving-brush on his chin abstractedly.

The windows, fourteen or fifteen feet above the ground, overlooked the extensive vegetable garden of the Rose and Crown. Below them, jutting out from the side wall of the house, was a small shed with a sloping, tarred roof. Between the shed and the fence of the vegetable garden, a cinder path ran to a decrepit-looking gate, leading into a narrow lane. Any average person so disposed could easily scale the gate, climb onto the roof of the shed, and, standing, reach one of the window-sills and pull himself up and into the room. Lowe always slept with his windows open, so the operation would have been comparatively noiseless. It would be quite safe to enter, attach the tubing to the jet, and lead the other end to the bed, closing the windows after escaping. Yes, Lowe mused as he applied some more lather to his chin, that was undoubtedly how it had been done. And it had been nearly successful, too.

When he had shaved and dressed, he descended to the coffee room, and was met at the door by White. 'The press is here in full force,' whispered his secretary. 'The place is simply teeming with reporters.'

'I thought it wouldn't be long before they put in an appearance,' remarked the dramatist.

'I didn't disturb you, but breakfast has been ready for some time,' went on White. 'I'll tell them to bring it in.' He stopped as he caught sight of Lowe's pale face. 'Good God!' he exclaimed in sudden alarm. 'What's the matter? Are you ill?'

'I'm not feeling too fit,' the dramatist admitted. 'It's nothing to worry about, though. I'll have some coffee, but otherwise I'll give breakfast a miss this morning. Gas is bad for the digestion.'

'What on earth are you talking about?' demanded the astonished White.

'Gas,' said Lowe with a smile, and proceeded to enlighten him as to the reason for his pale face and blue-shaded eyes.

White's expression as he listened grew horrified. 'What a diabolical scheme!' he exclaimed at the conclusion.

'We're dealing with a diabolical person,' said his employer gravely. 'However, all's well that ends well. Though the boots-man will, I'm afraid, remain to the end of his life under the impression that I tried to commit suicide, and I'm perfectly certain that nothing will ever shake that conviction.'

He entered the coffee room while White went to order breakfast, and was instantly surrounded by half a dozen varying types of humanity who had been consuming coffee and bacon and eggs at the long table in the centre. Lowe was known by sight to nearly all of the reporters on the London dailies, and their number was well represented at the Rose and Crown. He felt as little desire for cross-examination on the subject of the crimes that had rendered Stoneford such a centre of interest, and turned them all over to Inspector Rooper, despite their wailing protests that they had already seen that officer of the law. It was impossible to stop in the coffee room with any degree of comfort, and, without waiting for White's return, the dramatist fled hastily, found his hat and overcoat, and, concluding that a walk would do him a lot of good, hurriedly left the environs of the Rose and Crown.

The morning was clear and frosty, with a white sprinkling on hedge and tree. After making sure that none of the collection of copy-hunters had followed him, Lowe made his way round to the narrow lane from which the cinder path led across the vegetable garden. It was, he thought, unlikely that the night marauder would have left any trace, but there was just a chance that he might, and Lowe was not going to let the faintest opportunity slip through his fingers.

There was nothing in the lane, and, coming to the gate that separated it from the cinder path, the dramatist found that it was unlocked. Passing through, he walked up the little track between the vegetable-beds, his eyes keenly scrutinizing the ground at his feet. But the clinker ashes and cinders of which it was composed showed nothing. A regiment of soldiers might have passed that way without leaving any trace.

It was not until he reached the lean-to shed that he found anything to confirm his theory of how the unknown had managed to flood his bedroom with gas, and then it was nothing more than a few splinters of wood broken away from the woodwork, and one or two scratches on the tarred felt of the roof. They were fresh, however, and convinced Lowe that he had been right in his surmise as to which way the man had come.

Nobody had seen him come round to the shed, and since he was not particularly anxious to meet anyone just then, he left the same way as he had come, and set off at a brisk pace up the coombe towards the open moor. He walked almost as far as Princetown and back, and the keen, fresh air drove the last remaining fumes of gas from his system. By the time he once more reached the Rose and Crown — towards half-past two — he was feeling very nearly his normal self.

Dr. Macaulay was coming out of the garage with a couple of tins of petrol for his Ford, and he stopped Lowe with a cheery greeting. 'The inquest on Jensen has been feexed for eleven o'clock tomorrow,' he said after they had exchanged one or two commonplace remarks. 'They're holding it in the dining room at Ridgeway Manor. I expect ye'll find yer subpoena waitin' fer ye.'

'I don't suppose it will take very long,' answered Lowe. 'The police are sure to ask for an adjournment pending further evidence.'

'Aye.' The doctor nodded. 'Ye know there'll be quite an epidemic of inquests round these parts during the next week. Have you hit on anything that's likely to throw light on the culprit?'

Trevor Lowe shook his head. 'Nothing, I'm afraid. However, I haven't given up hope. Have the reporters been worrying you?'

Dr. Macaulay made a gesture of annoyance. 'Worrying me!' he repeated. 'Why, mon, they've pestered me life out eever since early this morning. Every time I came out of a patient's house, I found one or other of 'em waiting to question me.'

The dramatist laughed. 'I referred them all to Rooper,' he said, 'but I expect they'll be after me again as soon as I appear at the Rose and Crown.'

The doctor drove off, and Lowe, feeling decidedly hungry, entered the inn and made his way to the coffee room. White was reading a magazine by the fire, but otherwise the place was deserted.

'Hello!' said Lowe. 'What happened to our friends of the press?'

His secretary grinned. 'After trying to pump me for information all the morning, they've now gone along to the various scenes of the crimes,' he answered. 'How are you feeling now, sir?'

'Much better, and ravenously hungry. I suppose you've had lunch?'

White nodded. 'Yes, but they're keeping yours hot.'

The dramatist rang the bell, and intimated to the smiling waitress who answered that he would like food in large quantities.

'Oh, by the way,' said White, feeling in his pocket, 'the constable left this for you almost directly after you'd left.' He handed Lowe a piece of blue paper. Glancing at it, the dramatist saw that it was the subpoena for the inquest, and slipped it into his pocket.

He ate a substantial lunch, and afterwards went in search of the landlord. To that worthy man he intimated that it was desirable that some other sitting room should be found for himself and White, explaining the difficulties of sharing the coffee room with the army of news-gatherers. His arguments, reinforced by the casual display of a five-pound note, appeared to convince his host of the necessity of a private sitting room, and half an hour later Lowe and White found themselves installed in a small room behind the bar.

Having given orders that, with the exception of Inspector Rooper or Major Strickland, he was not at home to anybody, Lowe began to settle himself down for an afternoon of quiet thought. White, whose ankle was still painful and rendered him temporarily *hors de combat,* eventually fell asleep; but Lowe remained wakeful, his pipe belching forth clouds of smoke, his eyes closed, and his mind extremely alert, sorting and resorting the pieces of the puzzle that were in his possession.

Tea-time came without his having arrived at any definite conclusion. So far as he could see, there was a complete dearth of clues. There was simply nothing to get hold of. Whoever was responsible for the orgy of crime that had swamped the little village of Stoneford, he was a genius at covering up his tracks — or, rather, in not making any tracks to cover up.

The rosy-cheeked waitress was just clearing the tea away when Major Strickland arrived. His merry, florid face wore a worried look as he shook hands with Lowe and ordered a whisky and soda.

'Well, any news?' he asked as soon as the drink was brought and they were alone.

'So far as I'm concerned, none,' answered the dramatist.

Strickland grunted gloomily and gulped half his whisky. 'Unless something comes to light soon, I shall have to call in Scotland Yard. I don't want to do that if I can help it. I should like to bring this case to a successful conclusion without them. You know, prestige and all that sort of thing. But if I leave it too long before calling for help, they'll put over the usual bunk about being asked to solve a problem when all the clues are cold.'

'I don't see why you should be worrying yet,' remarked Trevor Lowe. 'After all, it's not so very long since the murders were actually committed.'

'I know that, but now that these confounded reporters have turned up, it'll be in all the papers. If something doesn't happen soon, they'll be asking why the Yard wasn't called in to tackle a big business like this. I know 'em.'

'I doubt if the Yard could have done any more than has been done,' said Lowe. 'Inspector Rooper can hardly be expected to produce the murderer out of his hat.'

'Personally, I'm perfectly satisfied,' said Major Strickland hastily. 'Only, if anything should happen to go wrong, and the murderer remains undiscovered, I shall get hauled over the coals for not asking for assistance.' He swallowed the remainder of his drink. 'You see my position, don't you?'

Trevor Lowe nodded. 'Yes, and the only

thing I can suggest is that you wait for another couple of days, and if nothing has been done by then you call in the Yard.'

Before Strickland could reply, there came a tap on the door, and in answer to the dramatist's invitation the waitress entered, holding in her fingers a slip of white pasteboard. 'There's a gentleman inquiring for you, sir,' she said, and held out the card.

Lowe took it, looked at it, and raised his eyebrows in surprise. 'Ask him to come in,' he said; and when the woman had departed: 'Somebody has apparently saved you the trouble of calling in Scotland Yard, Strickland. Detective Inspector Shadgold is here now, asking to see me.'

15

Jensen's Real Identity

Shadgold's burly form loomed in the doorway of the little sitting room. The Scotland Yard man's face was a bright crimson from the frosty air, and his breath came out in clouds of steam as though the fieriness of his face had set him alight inside. He gave a grunt at seeing Lowe that might have been pleasure or anything, and, advancing, gripped the dramatist's hand in a vice-like clasp.

'How are you, Mr. Lowe?' he said breathlessly. 'Left London this morning. Thought I was never going to get here. Outlandish hole.'

'I'm very glad to see you, Shadgold,' said the dramatist. 'But may I ask exactly why you've come?'

The inspector divested himself of his huge coat, tipped his hard bowler hat onto the back of his bullet head, and held out his hands to the fire. 'Came down about this Jensen business,' he replied shortly. 'Got your letter asking for information. Cabled to America. Got their reply this morning, and came along by the first available train. Devilish rotten one, too!'

'But why all the fuss and excitement?' asked Trevor Lowe curiously.

'You'll see why when I tell you who Jensen was,' grunted Shadgold. He settled his burly form in a chair by the fire and looked from one to the other. 'Ever heard of 'Scarlet' O'Hara?' he asked.

Trevor Lowe started, and his eyes narrowed. 'You mean the Chicago gangster?' he inquired.

'That's the feller,' said the Scotland Yard man. 'And that's also who your Elmer N. Jensen was!'

Major Strickland drew in a long breath. 'You mean that Jensen was once an American gangster?' he asked incredulously.

Shadgold nodded. 'He was. And he was more than that. He was one of the most notorious gang leaders in Chicago. The exploits of the O'Hara gang kept the circulation of the newspapers sky-high for over two years.'

'But how on earth did he get here?' said the chief constable. 'Why did he come and settle down in a little village like this?'

'It's a long story,' answered Shadgold, 'but I can assure you that the central office of the New York police are intensely interested to hear all about him. That's why I've come down.'

'Let's hear the whole story from the beginning,' suggested Trevor Lowe; and, with a nod of assent, Shadgold drew a bunch of papers from his pocket.

'All right,' he said, 'but I warn you that it's going to take a long time. It'll be dry work talking, too,' he added.

The dramatist smiled and took the hint. Ringing the bell, he ordered a bottle of whisky and a siphon of soda. When these had been brought, and the inspector supplied with a hissing tumbler, he began.

'As soon as I got your letter, Mr. Lowe,' he said, 'asking for information concerning Jensen, I cabled to America, giving your description of the man and particularly mentioning the heart-shaped scar on the right wrist — '

160

'Scar!' interrupted Strickland. 'That's the first time I've heard of any scar.'

'It was there all the same,' said Lowe. 'Red heart-shaped mark like a burn about halfway up the right forearm. I noticed it when I was looking at the body.'

'It's a good job you did,' said Shadgold, 'for it was that scar that made the New York police sit up and take notice.' He selected a cablegram from his bunch of papers and handed it to the dramatist. 'This was the reply I got to my inquiry.'

Lowe glanced at the message and then read it aloud.

CENTRAL DETECTIVE BUREAU, NEW YORK.

Reply to your inquiry 10237. Message begins. Description of Elmer N. Jensen tallies with Chicago gang leader O'Hara, alias 'Scarlet' O'Hara. Was given free pardon 1926 for turning state evidence against the Burke gang. Disappeared shortly after, and since no trace. Scanlon, O'Hara's right-hand man, also disappeared. Believed to have fled the country together. O'Hara wanted for murder of banker, Illinois, 1927.

Shall be glad of any information concerning this man. Message ends.

WILLIAM L. PHELPS (Captain).
'As soon as we got that,' said Shadgold as Lowe handed the cable back, 'we looked up the record of international criminals, and found a full report of O'Hara's activities, together with a photograph and description.' He produced a small square of pasteboard. 'Here's the photograph. Perhaps you can identify it as that of Jensen.'

Major Strickland rose as Lowe took the faded photograph and looked over his shoulder. It was a badly taken picture, but sufficiently clear for them to recognize it.

'Yes, that's Jensen right enough,' the dramatist remarked.

'Not the slightest doubt of it,' substantiated the chief constable.

'Well, that's a photograph of Scarlet O'Hara,' said Shadgold, 'so there's no mistake about them being one and the same man.' He fumbled again with his papers. 'Now I'll give you the official resume of his career, which was sent from America at the time.'

He took a drink of whisky and cleared his throat. 'There seems some little doubt as to his origin,' he began, 'but it is believed that his father was an Irish-American, Kearney O'Hara, a clerk in the Consolidated Bank of New York. O'Hara's criminal activities began at the age of twenty-two, when he received a sentence of three years for the attempted murder of a band leader in a nightclub. On his release he drifted amongst bad company, and after several further sentences for petty theft and robbery with violence, went to Chicago and formed the O'Hara gang.'

Shadgold paused and turned over several typed sheets. 'The list I have here,' he continued, 'of his various exploits, would take too long to go through. He appears, however, to have been a bright beauty, and under his leadership the gang became notorious. That, of course, was in the early days before gangs became so common in Chicago that the population now consists of nothing but crooks and police officers. At that time there were only two, O'Hara's lot and another almost as notorious led by a man named Burke.

'In 1926 O'Hara was caught during the smashing of the Chicago Joint Stock Bank, and in order to save his own skin he gave away Burke and most of the members of his own gang. Burke was executed with several of his confreres, and for this O'Hara received the state's pardon. He and his chief lieutenant, Mark Scanlon, disappeared, and it was believed that they'd fled the country and gone abroad.

'A year later, however,' Shadgold continued, 'a bank was broken into in Illinois, and the manager, who lived over it, was shot dead while trying to defend his property. Some fingerprints found on the premises turned out to be O'Hara's, and a search was instituted for him. He was never found, though the police of all countries were advised. The New York detective bureau were under the impression that he'd managed to escape to England, hence their communication with the Yard, and the very voluminous records that accompanied it. Of course, we did our best to find him at the time, but without result, and the records were filed and almost forgotten — until that cable from America stirred the whole thing up again.'

The Scotland Yard man drained the remainder of his whisky. 'I've no doubt they'll be very glad to hear that O'Hara's dead and the case is closed.'

'Begad, we seem to have been harbouring a nice specimen in our midst,' commented Major Strickland. 'An American gang leader in Stoneford. Good God, it's incredible!'

'And we're still faced with the problem of who killed him,' remarked Trevor Lowe. 'I must say that instead of making it easier, Shadgold's information increases the difficulties a thousandfold.'

'How?' asked White.

'Well, there are so many people who had a motive. The relations of Burke, for instance, and the remaining members of his and O'Hara's gang. A good few of them probably only got varying sentences, which will have by now expired, and any one of them may have traced him here and killed him for revenge.'

'Yes, that's a decided possibility,' agreed Shadgold. 'Look here, I've given you all the information I've got, but I know very little about what occurred here. Suppose you tell me the whole story. I don't want to butt in in an official capacity.' He looked across at Major Strickland and winked. 'Except to verify the fact that Jensen and O'Hara were one and the same. But I must say I'm interested.'

'I shall be only too pleased,' said Trevor Lowe heartily. 'You may be able to hit on something that we've overlooked.' He filled his pipe and, having lighted it, sank back comfortably in his chair. 'These are the facts up to date. See what you can make of them.'

Without omitting anything, he proceeded to relate the entire series of events, from the time the body of Jensen had been found under the heap of gravel to the last attempt on his own life while he slept. Shadgold listened intently. From force of habit, his fingers hovered round his breast pocket, and White grinned, for he guessed that the burly inspector was itching to produce the familiar black notebook.

Major Strickland stared in amazement as Lowe related the incident of the gas, for it was the first time he had heard anything about it, but he made no comment at the time.

'And that's the whole thing in a nutshell,' the dramatist concluded. 'Not a solitary clue to go on except that shred of grey woollen cloth; and unless we search the wardrobes of every inhabitant within a radius of fifty miles, that won't help us. Even if we did, it's a million chances to one against our finding anything.'

Shadgold wrinkled his bushy brows. 'I wonder how Jensen came into possession of those diamonds,' he said thoughtfully. 'I've got nothing about those in my records.'

'Probably he acquired those after he left America,' said Lowe. 'And that may help us, because if his murderer was someone who had known him in America, and those stones didn't come into his possession until after he left the country, the killer wouldn't have known anything about them.'

'It's all very complicated,' muttered the Scotland Yard man. 'Who's this woman that he passed off as his daughter, and why did he adopt her?'

'That's one of the minor mysteries about this case that we've got to solve,' answered Trevor Lowe. 'At the moment the pieces of the puzzle are scattered anyhow, and try how you will you can't put them together to make a coherent picture. There's one piece missing — a big piece — and until we find that, we shan't get the others to fit.'

'You mean — ' began the chief constable, and Lowe interrupted him.

'I mean,' he said, 'that we've got to find the motive not only for the murder of Jensen, but for Sedgwick's death as well. Once we find that — a motive that covers the two crimes — it shouldn't be so very difficult to lay our hands on the murderer.'

16

The Man Who Planned

The man who sat in front of the dying fire smoking thoughtfully was frowning. Things had not gone as well as he had hoped, and he was a little worried. It was not his conscience that was troubling him, though it well might have been, for the hand that removed the cigarette from his thin lips was red with the blood of three men, and had turned on the gas-tap that had so nearly cut short the promising career of Trevor Lowe.

Several things were worrying him, the predominant one being the whereabouts of the diamonds. What had that devil, O'Hara, done with them? The woman did not know. He had thought that she would, but had learned since that she had been speaking the truth. That business had been a sheer waste of time.

He flung the end of his cigarette into the fire and lit another. What troubled him was that he could not make up his mind as to his next move. The stones that he wanted were probably at Ridgeway Manor, but even of that he could not be sure. And even if they were, unless he knew exactly where they were hidden, it would be next to impossible to get hold of them. Burgling the place would be far too risky.

He muttered an oath. What a fool he had been to have killed Jensen before he had forced him to reveal what he had done with the stones. It would all have been so easy if he had not let his anger get the better of him. However, it was no good worrying about that now. Jensen was dead, and Sedgwick was dead — Sedgwick hadn't known anything, anyway — and the only thing to do was to make the best of it.

It was a nuisance having that interfering dramatist hanging around. Why in hell couldn't he stick to his job instead of poking his nose in other people's business? Without his damned cleverness, Jensen's murder would have passed as the accident he had intended it to. What a pity that the gas hadn't done its work. It would have served the man right. Damn him.

The man before the fire stretched out his legs and shifted uneasily in his chair. These disjointed thoughts were getting him nowhere. Why couldn't he concentrate on the thing that really mattered — the diamonds? They were what he wanted, and the trouble was how the devil he could get hold of them.

His brows drew down lower over his eyes as he forced his brain to work. They might not be in the house at all. O'Hara might have taken the precaution of depositing them at a bank or safe deposit, but this possibility didn't tally with what he knew. To do what he had intended doing, O'Hara would surely have kept them somewhere where he could lay his hands on them at once. They *must* be somewhere at Ridgeway Manor. How the hell was he going to find out *where*?

For two hours he sat cudgelling his brains to try and hit on a plan, but without success. The fire was out except for a spark when he was roused by the cold, and getting up hastily he threw on some more coal. Perhaps a drink would stimulate his dulled brain. He poured himself out a stiff whisky

171

from the bottle on the table and swallowed it at a gulp. Whether it would help him to find the plan he sought or not, it at least had the effect of putting fresh warmth into his chilled body.

He raked out the dead ashes from under the coal he had put on and stirred the fire, and going over to the window looked out. The night was dark and cold and uninviting, and dropping the curtains he shut it out. Restlessly he began to pace up and down, still worrying for the solution that eluded him. It was an impossible situation. Practically under his hand was a fortune, and he could not take it. Up and down, up and down he walked from the door to the covered window, his head sunk on his chest. There must be a way of finding out where those diamonds were, if only he could think of it. If only he could concentrate instead of letting his mind flit from one subject to another.

He was tired, that's what it was. The day had been a very heavy one, and he had had to be constantly on the lookout for fear of making a slip that would give him away. Yes, that's what it was — he was so tired that his weary brain refused to function. Perhaps it would be as well to go to bed and shelve the problem until the morrow. It was useless thinking round in circles like this.

And yet time was a factor that he had to reckon with. Somebody — the police or that interfering amateur, Lowe — might find the diamonds before he did. And then, goodbye to them.

Wearily he stopped by the table and helped himself to another drink. Why the hell hadn't he made Jensen tell him before killing him? There he was again! Going right back to the beginning and going round and round and round. Better go to bed. After all, it was very late. He glanced at his watch and was surprised to see how late it really was. Nearly four o'clock, and he would have to be up early. He turned out the light and made his way slowly up the stairs to his room.

Undressing, he got into bed, but his mind was still so active that sleep would not come for a long time, and when it did it was broken and fitful. He was lying not in bed but on a pile of grey-green stones; huge stones that ground into his flesh and bruised his bones. For miles around him they stretched, acres of them under a blazing sun that scorched his unprotected head and burnt up his life's blood. He tried to roll away from the glare of that devilish light, but he could not. Suddenly he saw that it wasn't the sun at all that was hanging there above him in the pitiless sky, but a face. The face of Elmer N. Jensen. It grinned down on him with the lips curled back in a mirthless smile. And as he looked, the flesh of the face became mottled and congested, the tongue protruded from the half-open mouth, and instead of being *above* him it was *underneath* him. The stones had become a cushion, and with this he tried to shut out that horrible face; pressing the cushion hard down over it, pressing, pressing, pressing ...

He succeeded, and with a shout of triumph flung the cushion away — only to find that the face was still there, but changed. He had made a mistake. It *wasn't* Jensen's face at all. This face was splashed with crimson, and as he stared down at it in horror, he saw that it was the face of Sedgwick. Sedgwick? Of course it wasn't

Sedgwick. It was Box! Box, with his matted hair and his broken teeth. Box, who should be dead. Who *must* be dead. He had killed him. And yet here he was, glaring at him with hate-filled, bloodshot eyes. He shrieked aloud, putting out his hands to try and shut out the sight of that face, but it grew larger and larger ...

He woke, his face streaming with perspiration, to find the dawn had broken and the bedroom filled with the pale rays of the morning sun. He got up, and pouring some water from a carafe into a glass, drank it greedily.

He felt tired and unrested. That distorted dream had been very vivid. It was barely six, and he thought of going back to bed again; but the draught of cold water had thoroughly wakened him, and he decided that he might as well dress. He went into the bathroom, bathed and shaved, and did certain things that were necessary to his appearance. When he was dressed, he went downstairs and put the kettle on for some tea. The thought of the diamonds came back to him as he waited for it to boil.

There seemed only one way he could

hope to find them, and that was with a thorough search of Ridgeway Manor. But he could not do this while it was occupied. Was there any means by which the present occupants could be forced to leave?

He considered all ways — some of them wildly impracticable — but nothing like a workable scheme suggested itself. He made his tea, cooked himself some breakfast and set about preparing for his day's work, little knowing that a ready-made plan was to be presented to him for securing possession of the hidden stones without any effort of his own.

17

The Secret of the Study

The jovial landlord of the Rose and Crown was easily persuaded to find a room for Shadgold, and the burly inspector stayed the night, agreeing to accompany Trevor Lowe to the inquest on the following morning.

As the dramatist had foreseen, the proceedings were of not much account. Evidence of identification and the cause of death were taken by the fussy little coroner, who in private life occupied the position of grocer in Princetown, and Inspector Rooper gave a very guarded account of the finding of the body. The murders of Sedgwick and Box were touched upon lightly, and a request for an adjournment pending further evidence on the part of the police was granted. After a very long-winded speech of sympathy for the dead man's daughter by the coroner, the inquest was adjourned until that day week.

The coroner gathered up his notes and the jury dispersed, and by a quarter to twelve Lowe and Shadgold — White had been forced to remain at the Rose and Crown on account of his ankle, much to his disgust — found themselves alone in the big drawing room with Dorothy Jensen and Leyton.

The former was still looking rather white from her experience of the night before, but otherwise had completely recovered her usual cool, practical manner. 'Thank God that's over!' she said, helping herself to a cigarette from a box on a small table. 'I'm afraid I can't pretend to feel emotional about it all, Mr. Lowe.' She added the last remark with a half-smile as though in apology.

'It is quite understandable, Miss Jensen,' the dramatist assured her. 'By the way, didn't you tell me that you were expecting your — er — father's solicitor today?'

She nodded. 'Yes. He should reach here shortly after five o'clock if he catches the train he said he was catching,' she replied.

'I should like to see him when he does arrive,' said Lowe. 'There are several things

I want to talk to him about.' He paused, and then went on: 'When you were looking over the papers in the study the other morning before Inspector Rooper and I got here, did you remove any?'

Dorothy looked surprised.

'No,' she said. 'Why?'

'You're quite sure?' persisted the dramatist.

'Quite,' she replied emphatically.

'Nor you, Mr. Leyton?'

The secretary shook his head. 'No; we left them exactly as we found them. Why, what's the idea?'

'It struck me at the time that there were so few,' explained Lowe thoughtfully. 'Far less than one would have expected to find. Do you know of any other place where Jensen would be likely to keep documents?'

Dorothy shook her head. 'No. There's a small bureau in his bedroom,' she said. 'But I've looked through that, and there's nothing in it except notepaper and envelopes.'

Trevor Lowe frowned. That extraordinary absence of documents had been worrying him. There was a possibility, of course, that

Jensen had been one of those people who destroy everything except the absolutely essential, or that he had kept his more private possessions, including perhaps those mysterious uncut diamonds, at his bank. It was following up this line of thought that prompted his next question.

'Where did he bank?' he asked.

'At the Westminster Branch of the Capital and Counties,' answered Leyton, and added as if he had read the dramatist's thoughts: 'But if you're under the impression, Mr. Lowe, that he kept any papers there, I think you're mistaken. I used to do a lot of business with the bank for him, but it was mostly connected with his account and the transfer of securities. He had no private safe there.'

'Was the Capital and Counties his only bank?' asked the dramatist.

'So far as I know,' replied the secretary. 'I've never heard of any other.'

'But for all that, he may have used another without your knowledge,' said Lowe.

'Oh, quite!' agreed Leyton. 'I was by no means in his entire confidence. I don't think anyone was,' he added.

There was a momentary pause during which Shadgold cleared his throat impatiently, obviously not a little bored.

'Did you ever suspect that Jensen was not his real name?' said Lowe, suddenly breaking the silence.

Leyton raised his eyebrows. 'I never suspected it,' he answered, 'but it wouldn't surprise me.'

'Why did you ask that?' inquired Dorothy curiously.

'Because,' said the dramatist, 'we happen to have authentic information that it wasn't. Jensen's real name was O'Hara.' He looked across at Dorothy. 'Does that convey anything to you, Miss Jensen?'

She wrinkled her smooth brows in perplexity. 'No,' she said; 'I don't think I've ever heard the name before.'

'I didn't expect you would have.' Lowe smiled grimly. There was a wide gap between the notorious Scarlet O'Hara and this slim woman who was looking at him with questioning eyes — and yet not so wide after all, considering that the gangster had adopted her and passed her off as his

181

own daughter. Why had he done that? To Lowe's mind, that was the most inexplicable mystery of the whole mysterious business.

Dorothy's voice broke in on his thoughts. 'Who was O'Hara? I mean, what was he? Was he — ' She left the sentence unfinished, but Lowe knew what was in her mind.

He considered before answering. There could be no harm in telling her. The truth would not hurt her in any way, seeing that there had been no blood relationship between her and the dead man, nor even the smallest grain of affection.

He decided eventually to tell her what he had learned on the previous evening from Shadgold. She and Leyton listened intently, while in a few brief sentences Lowe sketched O'Hara's career.

'So that was the man who for years let me think he was my father,' was Dorothy Jensen's low-voiced comment when he had finished. 'Mr. Lowe, although I would give almost anything in the world to know who my real parents were, you can't think how thankful I am that no trace of his blood runs in my veins.'

She stared at the floor for a moment, and

then raised her head with an expression of determination. 'Well, at any rate that settles one thing,' she said. 'Whether he left a will or not, I shall not touch a penny of his money now I know how it was come by. I should always feel that each one was stained with blood.' She shivered as though the room had grown suddenly cold.

'Do you think it possible, Mr. Lowe,' said Leyton, 'that this fellow Sedgwick could have been the man Scanlon who disappeared with Jensen? It seems quite likely — they were always as thick as thieves.' He laughed. 'That's rather a good simile under the circumstances.'

'The same idea struck me,' said Trevor Lowe, 'and it would certainly supply the link between them. Whoever killed Jensen killed Sedgwick as well, and with the same motive. What that motive was, we have yet to find out.' He turned to Dorothy. 'I should like to have another look at the study, Miss Jensen,' he said.

'Do just what you like, Mr. Lowe,' she answered. 'The whole house is at your disposal if you wish.'

The dramatist thanked her, and Leyton

offered to accompany him to the room, an offer which Lowe accepted.

When they arrived in the study, Shadgold put the question that had been hovering on his lips since he had heard Lowe's request. 'What's the idea?' he asked. 'What do you expect to find here?'

'Probably nothing,' answered Trevor Lowe, looking about him. 'What I'm hoping to find is someplace where Jensen could have concealed those diamonds. According to what the masked man said at the Black Moor Inn, there should be three hundred of them somewhere — or, rather, two hundred and ninety-seven, since we've already got three in our possession. Jensen may have deposited them with his solicitors, or rented a safe somewhere and put them there. I'm rather doubtful, though; and anyway, since we're here, there can be no harm in making sure that they're not in the house.' He glanced round the spacious book-lined room and then turned to Leyton. 'This house is of great age and, I believe, was in the possession of your family for centuries?'

The secretary nodded.

'I suppose you've never heard of any

secret hiding-places — false panels or priest holes or anything like that?'

'No,' answered Leyton, shaking his head. 'I've never heard of anything of the sort.'

'Well, in that case,' said Lowe, 'if there *is* anything of the sort, we must try and find it for ourselves, and I think the best thing we can do is to start with this room. Jensen, I understand, spent most of his time in here, and therefore, if he hid the diamonds anywhere in the house, it would most likely be here.'

Shadgold surveyed the room and shrugged his shoulders. 'Well, whereabouts in the room do we start?' he inquired.

Trevor Lowe waved his hand towards the tall bookcases that lined the walls, reaching almost to the ceiling. 'I suggest by making a careful examination of the books,' he replied. 'It's quite likely one of them may be a dummy. It's quite a common thing for a man to have a steel box made in the representation of a book, and when it's thrust in with others it's almost impossible to tell the difference.'

The Scotland Yard man gave a grunt. 'It's going to take some time to go through all these. There must be thousands of them.'

'Two thousand, six hundred and forty-five to be exact,' said John Leyton. 'Jensen, I believe, added a few novels, but that's what there used to be.'

'It may take some time, Shadgold,' said the dramatist with a smile, 'but then nothing worthwhile was ever accomplished without a little trouble. Besides, there are three of us, so it shouldn't take so very long after all. You and I can take the lower shelves as high as we can reach, and Leyton can use that ladder and account for the others.' He pointed to a light librarian's step-ladder that stood in a corner.

'I only hope the trouble will be worth it,' muttered Shadgold as he removed his coat preparatory to making a start, 'though I fully expect that the diamonds are safely locked up in a bank somewhere.'

They set to work, beginning on the wall by the door. Each volume, under Lowe's directions, was taken from its place and skimmed through, the space behind looked at, and the book returned. It was slow work, but by the time Dorothy appeared at two o'clock to say that lunch was ready and suggest that they should break off for something to eat, they had succeeded in thoroughly searching one wall, without, however, any result.

They ate a hasty meal and returned to their labours. The afternoon wore on, and it was with a sigh of relief that at a quarter to five Trevor Lowe replaced the last book — a sigh of relief mingled with disappointment, for they had found nothing.

'What do we do now?' inquired the Scotland Yard man sarcastically. 'Pull the house down brick by brick? I've still got a couple of hours left before catching my train back to town.'

Lowe lit a cigarette and frowned. 'Your trouble is impatience, Shadgold,' he said. 'I think the next thing we should do is have a look at the floor.'

Shadgold grunted something below his breath, but nevertheless assisted to roll back the square of carpet that occupied the centre of the room. The dramatist got down on his hands and knees and closely examined every inch of the polished floor. Not so much as a knot-hole escaped him, but at the finish he was forced to admit that nothing in the way of a possible hiding-place was there.

'I hope you're satisfied now,' panted Shadgold as he and Leyton replaced the carpet. 'The only place left in here is the ceiling, and thank God you can't reach that!'

This time Trevor Lowe made no reply. His narrowed eyes were travelling slowly about, resting momentarily on each object the room contained: the broad flat-topped writing-table between the big windows, the chesterfield and pair of armchairs drawn up before the fireplace, the small table at the back of the settee, the standard lamp, the large blue Ming vases, and clock on the broad mantelpiece. He made a mental inventory of them all. Where had Jensen put those diamonds? Supposing he himself had wanted to hide anything in that room. Where would he have chosen his hiding-place?

The least likely spot, of course, where anyone would ever dream of looking; but where was that? Certainly not the bookshelves — that would have been the most likely. Certainly not the floor. What about the settee or the chairs? Almost unconsciously he shook his head. Hardly likely — too difficult to get at. The clock? There was no room in that, and he had already looked into the vases that flanked it. Then where?

There were no pictures in the room. A large oval mirror occupied the bare space over the mantelpiece. A large oval mirror … Lowe's eyes opened wide. What was wrong about that mirror? Why, as he looked at it, did it jar on his senses?

He found the reason suddenly like a flash. It didn't fit in with the rest of the room — it was modern and new, out of keeping with the mellow furniture and old woodwork that time had blended to the atmosphere of the house. With a glint in his eyes, he swung round to Leyton. 'Has that mirror always been there?' he asked harshly.

'No,' answered the secretary. 'There used to be a picture there, but Jensen didn't like it — it was one of my ancestors — so he insisted on putting the mirror up in its place.'

'And hung it himself?' snapped Lowe.

Leyton looked surprised. 'Yes, now I come to think of it, he did,' he said. 'But — '

Trevor Lowe wasn't listening. 'Give me

the steps,' he said sharply. When they were brought over, he mounted them; and with the assistance of Shadgold, who had suddenly become galvanized into life, he lifted the heavy mirror down from its supporting chains. Carrying it over to the settee, he laid it face downwards and examined the back. His eyes gleamed with elation as he found that the thickness between the thin three-ply backing and the glass itself was over two inches.

'Help me get this back off, Shadgold,' he said, his voice vibrating with his excitement.

'Do you think — ' began the Scotland Yard man, but the dramatist interrupted him.

'I think I've found what we've been looking for,' he said, 'but we shall soon know for certain.'

And know they did. In a short while they had removed the tacks that held the back in position. Pulling out the oval of thin wood, Lowe pointed triumphantly at the row upon row of grey-green pebbles that were snugly packed between the glass and the backing that had kept it in place.

18

The Sealed Envelope

'Two hundred and ninety-seven.' Trevor Lowe added the last stone to the little pile that had risen up on the small table by the settee. 'Counting the one found under Jensen's body and the two in Sedgwick's cottage, that makes three hundred — the exact number mentioned by the masked man at the Black Moor Inn.'

'Well, you were certainly right, Mr. Lowe,' admitted Shadgold. 'Though now you've found 'em, I don't see that it's going to help us much in identifying the man who killed Jensen.'

'It's going to help a lot,' retorted the dramatist. 'Three hundred uncut diamonds must have been got from somewhere. They don't grow on gooseberry bushes. What we've got to do now is to find out how these came into Jensen's possession.'

'He may have bought 'em,' said the

Scotland Yard man. 'Perhaps he thought it was a way of investing his money.'

'Have you ever tried to buy uncut diamonds?' asked the dramatist.

Shadgold shook his bullet head. 'Never had the chance,' he answered gloomily. 'Scotland Yard doesn't pay enough for me to go in for collecting diamonds.'

'Well, if you had,' said Lowe, 'you'd find that it wasn't so easy. Whichever mine these came from would have a record showing to whom they were sold.'

'What about I.D.B.?' suggested Leyton.

'I don't think illicit diamond-buying is likely,' replied the dramatist; 'not in such large quantities as this, and certainly not from one mine, and these all appear to have the same origin.'

'Is it possible to tell?' asked Shadgold.

'Oh yes, quite possible.' Lowe picked up one of the dull little stones. 'An expert could tell you at once which mine these came from, and that must be our first line of inquiry. I know a man in Hatton Garden who will possibly be able to put us in touch with the information we want.'

Such an inquiry, however, was destined

to be rendered unnecessary, though Trevor Lowe was unaware of it when he spoke. Before the evening was over, they were to know exactly where those diamonds had come from, and to be practically certain of the name of the man who had killed Jensen and been responsible for the other crimes in the neighbourhood of Stoneford — though it was due to Trevor Lowe's cleverness that he was eventually caught and his identity revealed beyond doubt.

'We'd better find something to put these in,' said the dramatist, indicating the heap of stones, 'and turn them over to the police. As you're not officially interested in the case, Shadgold, they'd better go to Rooper. One thing, however, I should like done at once. Tell all the servants, and anybody else you can think of who's likely to gossip, that they've been found.' He looked at Leyton. 'I want the whole village to know, and add that I am taking charge of them for the next few days.'

The secretary looked surprised, but nodded without comment, and went in search of an attaché case in which to pack them.

'Why so keen about publicity?' asked

Shadgold curiously when Leyton had gone. 'I can't understand why you want it shouted from the house-tops. What's the idea?'

'By divulging that these diamonds have been found,' said Lowe, 'we may be provided with the only means we have of catching the murderer. A plan has just occurred to me — ' He broke off as Dorothy Jensen came in.

'Mr. Litchgrove, the solicitor, has just arrived,' she announced. 'I thought perhaps you'd like to be present and hear what he's got to say.'

'I most certainly should,' answered Trevor Lowe. 'Where are you having the interview?'

'In the drawing room.'

'Then we'll join you there in a few moments,' said Lowe.

Dorothy had scarcely left them before Leyton came back with the attaché case he had been to fetch, and Lowe carefully packed the grey-green stones away. When he had locked it and sealed it with some sealing-wax from the writing table, he pronounced himself ready to go and hear what information the lawyer had to give.

Mr. Litchgrove was a small, dried-up little man, rather like a decayed walnut, for his face was seamed with thousands of wrinkles. A sliver of side whiskers framed his sallow cheeks and, since the top of his head was almost completely bald, gave the effect of his hair having slipped from its rightful position probably due to too much brushing. He was regaling himself with a glass of sherry when they entered the drawing room — a task which he performed with an almost devotional air, as though he were about to utter a solemn incantation.

Dorothy introduced them, and Mr. Litchgrove set down his glass and wiped his thin lips with a handkerchief. 'Of course I've heard of Mr. Trevor Lowe,' he said, extending a thin hand in greeting, which reminded Lowe of a bundle of rather damp twigs. 'This terrible affair is a distressing business, Mr. Lowe — a most distressing business.' He cleared his throat and looked at his empty glass gloomily. Lowe wasn't quite sure whether he was referring to the death of Jensen or to the state of the glass, and evidently Dorothy was also a little hazy as to Mr. Litchgrove's exact meaning, for she hastened to offer him some more sherry.

'Thank you, thank you!' said the lawyer. 'An excellent wine, Miss Jensen — a very excellent wine. It is a great grief to me that I should be here under such sad circumstances.'

Lowe noticed that the circumstances had evidently not impaired Mr. Litchgrove's enjoyment of the good things in life, for he sipped the sherry with evident appreciation. 'You had, no doubt, many dealings with Mr. Jensen?' he suggested after a pause, during which he waited vainly for Mr. Litchgrove to say something.

'Several, several,' admitted the lawyer, lowering his voice. 'Mr. Jensen was a very good businessman, and had a shrewd eye for an investment.' He set down his glass and reached for a black bag that reposed on the floor beside him. 'His affairs are in perfect order — perfect order.'

'Did he make a will?' said the dramatist a trifle sharply. He had taken an intense dislike to Mr. Litchgrove.

The lawyer opened the bag carefully before replying and withdrew a bulky envelope, heavily sealed. 'I am under the impression that he did. He always gave me to understand that full instructions for the disposal of his estate were in here.' He tapped the envelope with a thin forefinger.

Trevor Lowe raised his eyebrows. 'Then you don't know the contents of that envelope?'

Mr. Litchgrove shook his head. 'I do not. It was delivered into my keeping, sealed as it is at present, by Jensen himself, with instructions that it was not to be opened except in the event of his death, and that then the contents were to be read by me to his daughter in the presence of a third party. I am here this evening to carry out those instructions.'

Lowe felt his pulse beating a trifle faster. What did the envelope contain? What light, if any, would it shed upon the murder? That it contained something out of the ordinary, something beyond a mere will, was obvious from the instruction the lawyer had received that it was not to be opened until after Jensen's death. Or was that just a whim? Lowe didn't think so. Jensen was scarcely likely to have issued those instructions out of sheer eccentricity.

The lawyer re-closed his bag and, resting the envelope on his knee, replaced it beside his chair. 'If you are agreeable, Miss Jensen,' he said, addressing Dorothy, 'I will proceed to open this envelope and acquaint you with the contents.'

She nodded. 'Please do,' she said a little breathlessly.

With maddening deliberation, Mr. Litchgrove felt in his pocket, produced a metal case from which he extracted a pair of gold-rimmed pince-nez, adjusted them to the bridge of his thin nose, and inserted his thumb delicately beneath the sealed flap of the envelope. With a little crackling sound the wax split, and the lawyer took out a thick wad of folded paper. Lowe saw that it was composed of several closely written sheets held together by a clip in the top left-hand corner. He had been right — there was more than a will.

Mr. Litchgrove laid aside the envelope and spread the manuscript out on his bony knees. It was then discernible that there were two documents — the sheets held together by the clip, and another consisting of a single sheet of thicker paper. Mr.

Litchgrove looked at it — looked again as though he was doubtful of the evidence of his own eyesight — and then in a thin, dry voice remarked: 'This appears to be his will, Miss — er — Jensen. It is most extraordinary — most extraordinary. I had no idea that Jensen was not his real name. However, that is immaterial. I will carry out my instructions and read the contents.'

He gave a little preliminary cough and then began: 'This is the last will and testament of me, James Addison O'Hara of the Laurels, Golder's Green, London, made this 27th day of September, 1929. I give and bequeath to Dorothy Ann Jensen, known as my daughter, everything of which I shall die possessed. Signed, James Addison O'Hara. Witnessed by Abel Minter and Alice Blint.'

Complete silence followed Mr. Litchgrove's reading of this short but pithy document. The lawyer looked over his glasses at Dorothy. 'I had no idea,' he said, 'that you were not Mr. Jensen's — er — Mr. O'Hara's daughter. However, nothing can alter the fact that you are his sole beneficiary under this will, and you will inherit his entire estate.'

Dorothy said nothing, but her eyes looked troubled. After a slight pause the little lawyer, prompted by Lowe, turned his attention to the remaining document that the envelope had held. 'This appears to be a statement of some kind,' he said. 'It is not headed in any way and begins quite abruptly.'

He leaned back, crossed his legs, and began to read aloud the following strange story.

19

The Story of the Diamonds

'There is a possibility that I may die, like any other man, in my bed from natural causes,' Mr. Litchgrove read. 'On the other hand, there is the possibility that my end may come suddenly and in a violent manner. In either case it is as well, for the benefit of the woman who has always believed herself to be my daughter, to place on record a few facts concerning myself, and incidentally herself, to set at rest any arguments or unpleasantness that may occur.

'As this document will never be read until I have ceased to exist, I can be quite frank. Let me start, therefore, by saying that my real name is James Addison O'Hara. Jensen was the name of my one and only friend, whose name I adopted on my arrival in England four years ago. He — the real Elmer N. Jensen — died in Chicago twenty-one years ago. He was a widower, and left behind him a baby girl, whom he made me swear on his death-bed that I would look after. I have kept my oath, partly because my friendship with Jensen is the only thing I can look back on with any pleasure, and partly because even then I saw a possibility of the child being made useful. I put little Dorothy Jensen in the care of an old nurse of my own until she was old enough to go to a convent.

'There is no need for me to set down here my life story — it is already recorded, I believe, with a wealth of detail at the Central Police Bureau, New York. My sole object in writing this document is to settle two points that may arise after my death and cause unnecessary trouble. One is the identity of the woman who has passed as my daughter and to whom I have left everything I possess. The other is the ownership of a number of uncut diamonds which will be found — unless I am lucky enough to be able to dispose of them before, which seems unlikely — concealed in the mirror in my study at Ridgeway.'

Trevor Lowe leaned forward interestedly as the lawyer paused to clear his throat.

'These stones,' Mr. Litchgrove continued reading, 'came into my possession while I was in Chicago and running the O'Hara gang. Scanlon, who was my right-hand man, had met a man called Menshaw who had told him a queer story, and he brought this fellow to me. Just before the outbreak of the war, in 1914, Menshaw had been working for a German mining syndicate. They were principally interested in copper, and his job had been a sort of roving commission — most of the time across the Orange River, in Great Namaqualand — German South-West, as it was then. Menshaw and a fellow called Selgz used to stray about there on the veldt for months at a stretch, looking for copper. He said he never found any, but eventually, by accident, he did find something.

'That part of Africa, Menshaw said, was like Salisbury Plain without the trees and without the roads, and multiplied until your multiplication gives out. One day the sun got Selgz and he pegged out. That settled Menshaw, and he decided to make tracks for Port Nesbit, the base they had started from.

'To cut a long story short, he lost himself in the middle of the prairie. However, he went on and on — like a flea on an eider-down that never stopped, to use his own expression — until the country changed and he came to a sort of ravine, running northwest and south-east, cut out of the scrub. What struck him first as funny about it was that the floor of it was covered thickly with sand and rubble.

'It was getting dark, however, and he was dog-tired, so, weeding out the rubble, he scooped together a heap of sand for a mattress and slept. When he awoke, the first thing that caught his eye was a little pile of grey-green stones lying in the hollow. They were diamonds. Looking around, he saw that the sand was full of them, and the reason for their presence was obvious. Some time or other there had been a river there, a split from the Orange, and down that river had gone for thousands of years part of the silt of the main stream. In the silt went the diamonds, until one fine day the river dried up.

Menshaw picked up as many of the larger stones as he could find room for in his knapsack, and set off on his way to find the fort. It was his intention when he got there to go back with a fleet of lorries and a mining concession. But he found that during his absence war had been declared.

'He was an Englishman, and it was with difficulty that he escaped being interned. There is no need for me to go into the details of what happened to Menshaw between that time and the time he met me. It is sufficient to say that he hadn't been able to get rid of any of those diamonds — at least, not at the price he wanted. It's not easy for people to sell diamonds who don't want to say where they got them, especially uncut stones. There were plenty of men who would have bought them at their own price, but Menshaw hadn't wanted to sell then.

'Things had, however, gone wrong with him, and he was pretty hard up when he met me. So he suggested, knowing that I was pretty conversant with the underworld, that I should try to get rid of them for him. As a matter of fact, I was on the point of leaving Chicago myself then, for there had been some trouble with the police. By giving them some information they wanted concerning one or two undesirable people, I had been given permission to leave the city. However, on hearing Menshaw's story, I decided to postpone my departure until the following day. I foresaw a chance of leaving with something worthwhile.

'I suggested that Menshaw should bring the diamonds to me that evening, and he agreed, arranging to pay me twenty percent of what I got for them. I made an appointment to meet him on a lonely stretch of road just outside Chicago at ten-thirty that night, and when he had gone I unfolded my plan to Scanlon. He jumped at the idea. He was a good fellow, and I was taking him with me when I left. We kept the appointment, cracked Menshaw over the head, secured the diamonds, and set off for Illinois, where we had decided to remain for a time.

'We knew Menshaw wouldn't dare inform the police about the loss of the stones, so we felt quite safe, and Scanlon had a plan for getting rid of them. He had been brought up in England and knew a fellow there who was in the lapidary trade. It was his idea to get to England, have the stones cut, and then sell them one by one. It wouldn't be so difficult to sell cut stones. But although the police had given me permission to clear out of Chicago, they had taken everything I possessed, including my money, and I was pretty hard up.

'We decided to augment the exchequer by robbing the Central Bank. Everything would have been all right if the manager, who lived on the premises, hadn't woken up and surprised us. I only meant to knock him out, but I must have hit him too hard in my excitement. However, we got away, and with enough money to keep us going for a long time.

'And now the usefulness of Jensen's daughter manifested itself. She had never been told that I was not her real father, and, taking the name of my dead friend, I called for her at the convent and took her to England. Her presence was a safeguard to me, for the police, who were looking for me for the murder of the bank manager, never expected that I could suddenly have acquired a grown-up daughter, for it was known that women had never attracted me, and that I was unmarried.

'Scanlon changed his name to Sedgwick, and I took a house at Golders Green. The stock exchange had always interested me — I suppose I had the gambler's nature — and speculating with the money I had got from the Central Bank, I quickly doubled and trebled it. Sedgwick kept away from me for a time, for it was dangerous for us to be seen together. His lapidary friend was dead, so for the moment we could do nothing with the diamonds.

'This was immaterial, however, because I was making plenty of money, and had gone in for company promoting. A few years later I acquired Ridgeway Manor and came down to live at Stoneford. Sedgwick came with me, and I gave him a cottage on the estate. He had begun tentative negotiations to dispose of the stones, having found a man who was willing to buy them and cut them at a reasonable price, and no questions asked.

'I think I have made everything clear except the beginning of this narrative. I stated that I might suffer a violent death. I have very little grounds for making this assertion except a feeling that comes over me now and again when I am sitting in my study alone — that and the fact that Scanlon swears he saw Menshaw one day in London. However, in case anything should happen to me, I feel that some explanation is due to Dorothy. I have never liked her, and she takes no pains to hide her dislike of me. But since, when I die, no doubt the whole of my career will be made public, I feel a sense of duty to my dead friend, who was one of the straightest men I ever knew. I have therefore written this narrative to let his daughter know that none of my blood taints her veins, and also to save her the trouble and embarrassment of having to explain away those uncut diamonds.'

Mr. Litchgrove finished reading this strange and rather disjointed document, blew his thin nose vigorously, and in the ensuing silence wiped his glasses.

Trevor Lowe was the first to speak. 'That sheds a considerable light on the mystery,' he remarked. 'We now know where the diamonds came from and the name of their original owner.'

Dorothy Jensen shivered. 'It's all ... horrible,' she whispered. 'Although I can't say how thankful I am that I'm not his daughter.'

'O'Hara must have written this before he told you he wasn't your father,' said Lowe, and she nodded. 'It's curious what peculiar streaks there are in even the worst characters. Gangster, thief, and murderer though he undoubtedly was, O'Hara kept his word to his only friend. Psychologically that's one of the most interesting traits in his character.'

'Psychology be damned!' snorted Shadgold. 'We are still no closer to catching the man who killed him than we were before.'

'I'm not so sure of that,' said the dramatist. 'At least we can have a good guess at his name.'

'You mean this fellow Menshaw?' Shadgold frowned. 'I don't see that you've any very strong reason for supposing so except that Jensen — O'Hara — was in London and seemed to go in some fear.'

'We have more than that,' said Lowe. 'We were looking for a motive that would cover both crimes, and now we know for a fact that Sedgwick was Scanlon, and that both he and O'Hara were connected with the robbery of the diamonds. We've found it.'

'Hm, there is that,' grunted the Scotland Yard man. 'But it applies equally well to any of the gangsters O'Hara shopped and who may be free now.'

'But they wouldn't have known about the diamonds. Our killer knew all about them, and that definitely links Menshaw with the murders.'

Mr. Litchgrove nodded his small, bald head. 'That is logical,' he interposed.

'Even supposing it was Menshaw, I still don't see how you're going to catch him,' said Shadgold stubbornly.

Trevor Lowe rose to his feet and smiled. 'I've got a plan which I think may achieve that,' he said. 'If you'll walk back with me to the Rose and Crown, I'll tell you about it.'

He took his leave of Dorothy, Leyton and the little lawyer, who was staying at Ridgeway Manor for the night. During the walk back to the village, he outlined to Shadgold a scheme for catching the murderer of O'Hara, Sedgwick and Box with which even that rather sceptical official could find no fault.

20

The Ambush

Trevor Lowe was up early the following morning and had breakfasted and gone out long before Shadgold, who had decided after very little persuasion to stay on at Stoneford and see the result of the dramatist's plan for catching the unknown killer, had thought of getting out of his comfortable bed.

Lowe's first call was at the police station, where he held a long interview with Inspector Rooper that left that grizzled official in a state of mind that can only be described as hilarious. Immediately following that, Lowe put through a call to Major Strickland. His conversation with the chief constable was short and noncommittal, for it merely consisted of an appointment to meet the dramatist for lunch at the Rose and Crown at one-thirty.

Having completed these two pieces of

business, Lowe returned to the inn to find the Scotland Yard man and White at breakfast in the coffee room.

'Hello, where have you been?' asked White, looking up from buttering a large piece of toast.

The dramatist poured himself a cup of coffee and slowly began to fill his pipe. 'I've been spreading the news,' he said quietly. 'I've also arranged for Strickland to meet us for lunch, so that we can discuss the final details of our little trap.'

'I only hope we get the bird,' grunted Shadgold, reaching for the marmalade.

'I think we shall get the bird all right,' answered Lowe, 'and I'm inclined to believe that it will be a very fierce species.'

They had conducted the conversation in whispers, for at another table a group of newspaper men were eyeing them curiously.

Lowe saw their glances and smiled across genially. 'I've got some news for you, boys,' he said. 'A large collection of uncut diamonds has been found in the dead man's study at Ridgeway Manor, hidden in a mirror over the fireplace.'

In an instant there was a concerted rush, and Lowe was inundated by a volley of questions.

'Just a minute,' he protested good-naturedly, holding up his hand to check the babel. 'Don't all speak at once.'

Having succeeded in stemming the flood of volubility, he gave a clear and detailed account of the finding of the diamonds — omitting, however, to mention anything with regard to the document that Mr. Litchgrove had read. 'That's all I can tell you at the moment,' he ended.

'Where are the stones now?' inquired one of the reporters.

'In my possession,' answered the dramatist. 'Tomorrow morning they'll be taken up to London by Inspector Shadgold.'

He answered several other questions, and then the newspaper men went swarming out to send the information they had acquired to their various newspapers.

The rest of the morning passed dully enough. Dr. Macaulay dropped in for a few moments' chat on his way to his morning's round, and listened amazed at the latest development. 'Mon, I theenk ye are takin' a serious reesk in keepin' those stones in yer possession,' he said with a shake of his head. 'If it were me, I should place them in the hands of the police until your friend was ready to take them with him to Lunnon.'

'They'll be safe enough, Doctor,' said Lowe with a smile. 'I shall sleep with them under the bed, and I'm a light sleeper. I'd rather not trust them out of my possession.'

'Weel, yer know your own beesiness best,' replied Macaulay, but he was still shaking his head dubiously when he departed in his noisy little Ford.

Major Strickland arrived at lunchtime, red of face and puffing and blowing like a grampus. He greeted the dramatist with a string of questions, but Lowe steered him skilfully into the bar and drowned his volubility in old brown sherry.

By Lowe's orders, lunch had been laid in their private sitting room. When the waitress had brought in the simple meal and taken her departure, the dramatist looked at his three companions. 'Before I go into details of the various jobs we shall undertake to-night,' he said, 'I think I had better apprise Major Strickland here of the finding of the diamonds, which, up to the present, he knows nothing about.'

Shadgold nodded, his mouth full of roast beef; and Lowe, for the umpteenth time since he had taken those grey-green stones from their hiding-place, told the story of their discovery.

'And now,' he continued when he had finished and the chief constable had expressed his astonishment at the contents of the document written by O'Hara, 'I will outline my scheme for the capture of the killer. Shadgold is already aware of it, and although it may not come off, I think there's a very good chance that it will. If it does, it will save a considerable amount of time and trouble.'

He stopped and turned the conversation to ordinary channels while the smiling waitress cleared away the luncheon things and brought coffee. Then, passing his cigar-case to Major Strickland and Shadgold, he filled and lit his pipe and proceeded as if there had been no break.

'I think there can be little doubt,' he said, 'that the man we are after is Menshaw. Our difficulty is that we don't know what he's like or anything about him, except that it's a practical certainty that he's somewhere in the immediate neighbourhood. Now my plan is this: Menshaw is obviously after those diamonds. The fact that he took the trouble to waylay Miss Jensen and question her at the Black Moor Inn proves that, and he's not likely to go without them if he can see a possible chance of getting hold of them. If he'd known where they were hidden, he'd have made some attempt for them before; possibly broken into Ridgeway Manor.

'Now, I've taken considerable pains to broadcast the fact that the diamonds have been found and that they're in my possession. I've added that tomorrow morning Shadgold is taking them up to London with him. This piece of information is almost bound to reach the ears of our man, and if it does he'll realize that his one chance of laying his hands on those stones will be tonight. I've told everybody that I'm sleeping with them under my bed, and since he's already made one visit to my room — luckily unsuccessfully — by way of the shed in the garden, I feel fairly confident that he'll pay another.'

'It seems quite a feasible scheme,' said the chief constable. 'There's only one thing. Supposing this fellow we're after doesn't get to hear about the diamonds. What then?'

Lowe shrugged his shoulders. 'In that case our scheme will fail,' he replied, 'and we shall have to resort to something else. As he will, however, undoubtedly be on the alert for any news concerning Ridgeway and the diamonds, I think the possibility that he won't become aware of them having been found is remote. However, we must take the risk of that.'

Throughout the afternoon they sat round the fire discussing the arrangements for the night, and it was past five before Major Strickland took his departure, promising to return later in the evening.

At eight o'clock, Inspector Rooper came across from the police station to report that all Lowe's orders had been attended to. He had scarcely left before the chief constable reappeared after an early dinner. The rest of the evening dragged slowly to an end, especially to White, who was consumed with excitement. His ankle had prevented him from leaving the inn, and so the anodyne of exercise was denied him.

They heard the landlord bolt and chain the front door, and then, after wishing them good night, make his way ponderously upstairs to bed. Lowe had already informed him that Major Strickland would be stopping very late, and had undertaken to re-lock up after he had gone.

At twelve o'clock the dramatist rose, and, knocking the ashes out of his pipe, turned to Shadgold. 'I think it's time we took up our positions,' he said. 'White, you go to your room, light the gas, and go through the pretence of undressing. I shall do the same in case our friend is watching outside. Rooper will have stationed his men by now. They have instructions not to challenge anybody until they hear me whistle. We want to catch this fellow red-handed so that there's no possibility of a mistake.'

He turned out the light in the sitting room and led the way upstairs, followed by the others. White took leave of them outside the dramatist's door and went along to his own room. Accompanied by Shadgold and Major Strickland, Lowe entered his bedroom.

'Don't let yourselves be seen near the window,' he warned as he lit the gas, 'and I don't think we'd better talk.'

The Scotland Yard man and the chief constable sat on the edge of the bed while Lowe went through the pantomime of undressing, crossing and recrossing in front of the window. Presently he reached up and turned out the gas, coming over to the bed and slipping on his dressing gown.

'Shadgold,' he said, 'get in the shadow of that wardrobe; and Strickland, you'd better take up your position under the bed. I'm going to lie down and pull the clothes over me so that it will look as though I really am asleep in bed.'

He suited the action to the word, and in the darkness the other two took up their appointed places. A silence fell upon the room, broken only by the rather heavy breathing of Detective Inspector Shadgold. Trevor Lowe, his eyes half-closed, lay watching the window.

The trap was set. Who would walk into it?

21

The Getaway

Night brooded darkly over the little village of Stoneford. Heavy clouds obscured the stars and a thin, wetting drizzle of rain fell steadily. Every now and again a gust of chill wind whined round the Rose and Crown.

Save for the faint blue lamp outside the police station, there was no light anywhere, for the villagers were early risers and had all long since gone to bed. The cracked bell in the steeple of the church chimed one, but not a soul stirred in the main street, and everywhere that peculiar silence that is the prerogative of the country reigned supreme.

Presently, far up the narrow lane that lay at the back of the inn, came a faint sound mingled with the hissing of the rain and the sighing of the wind — the faint, almost imperceptible crunch of a stealthy footfall. It came again; and then, a patch of darker shadow against the gloom, a figure showed — a crouching, creeping figure clad in a long coat and showing little of its face. Slowly this sinister shape born of the night moved forward, until it reached the gate that opened onto the strip of cinder path crossing the kitchen garden at the back of the Rose and Crown.

Here the shrouded figure paused, listening and looking up towards a black window that, dark and lightless, was sited immediately above the sloping roof of the lean-to shed. Apparently satisfied, the shadowy form began swiftly to climb the gate into the garden beyond. Avoiding the crunching cinders and walking on the soft earth at the side, it advanced towards the shed. Here again it paused, eyeing with satisfaction the half-open window above. Then, making scarcely a sound, it climbed up onto the roof.

To pull itself up from thence to the sill offered no difficulty. The muffled shape felt in its pocket and took out something that it held for a second in its right hand. The hand disappeared within the window, and there came the faint tinkle of broken glass. It was scarcely audible, but the man on the window-sill smiled grimly behind the silken handkerchief that covered his face. A second passed, another, and still the figure clung to its precarious perch, motionless.

At the expiration of a minute, it began to move. Cautiously the window was raised to its full extent, and with infinite care the man slipped into the darkened room beyond. Just inside he stood, hardly breathing, listening; but the only sound that broke the stillness was the steady breathing of the figure in the bed. The masked intruder drew a torch from his pocket, and a fan-shaped bar of light cut through the gloom. It flashed across the bed and settled on a small table at the head.

A sibilant breath drawn between clenched teeth came from the holder of the light as his eyes fell on a brown leather attaché case standing on the table. In two noiseless strides he reached it and picked it up. It was locked, but, gently shaking it against his ear, he smiled with satisfaction as he heard something inside rattle.

The light of the torch went out, and it was hurriedly restored to his pocket and replaced by a length of cord. Working swiftly, he passed the cord through the handle of the case and knotted it round his neck so that the case hung suspended. The next instant he had returned to the window and was outside the sill. Nothing moved from within the room.

The man in the bed lay like a log, and the faintly sweet, sickly smell that permeated the atmosphere oozed out into the clear air of the night. The marauder, the bag swinging against his chest, lowered himself carefully to the roof of the shed, and from there to the ground.

He was halfway down the cinder path when a noise behind him stopped him suddenly, bringing him to a halt with a jerk and a catching breath. The sharp, shrill blast of a whistle rang out with a startling clearness!

Instantly the little vegetable garden of the Rose and Crown woke to life. From the shadows of the surrounding hedges appeared men like jack-in-the-boxes — big, burly men who converged on the crouching figure on the cinder path. The man in the mask glared from side to side like a trapped animal, and his hand flew to his pocket. There was a flash and a report, and one of the men who were bearing down upon him gave a choking cry and collapsed in his tracks.

Again the automatic spoke, and Inspector Rooper cursed as a red-hot pain seared the upper part of his right arm. With a snarl, the night intruder swung round and dashed for the little gate. Two plainclothes men tried to stop him, but he turned on them like a maniac and lashed out with the butt of his pistol. Before they could recover, he was through the gate and speeding down the lane.

A car stood waiting where it joined the road, and into this the masked man flung himself, stamping furiously on the self-starter pedal. The engine throbbed to life and the car shot forward. The man at the wheel heard the shouts behind him, but he only smiled as he thrust hard on the accelerator. The car took a corner on two wheels and skidded into the main road. A figure loomed up out of the darkness and stepped into the glow of the headlights, but the driver never slackened his mad speed, and the policeman jumped aside only just in time to avoid being run down.

On through the night sped the car, and the man at the wheel laughed aloud at the success of his getaway. He'd beaten them. All of them. The policemen were no match for him. Even Trevor Lowe wasn't so very clever after all. Not as clever as he was. The blood tingled in his veins, and his eyes sparkled as he wallowed in the pleasure of his own self-esteem. He had got the diamonds. The bag, still hanging round his neck and resting on his chest, was very comforting.

He had prepared for just such an emergency as this, and he congratulated himself on his good generalship. In Exeter there was a cosy little flat rented in the name of Colonel Wyatt, a convenient bolt-hole where one could thoroughly change one's appearance before quickly slipping out of the country. Everything was waiting for him there — money, a complete outfit, passport, everything he needed. He chuckled again, shaking with laughter. Oh yes, he had thought of everything. He wasn't the type to be caught napping.

Reaching a darkened stretch of road that led up to the open moor, he brought the car to a halt under the shadow of a hedge.

Taking a small case from one of the door pockets, he produced from it a mirror, a razor and a pair of scissors, and in the light of the dashboard lamp, proceeded to make such changes in his appearance as he deemed necessary. When he had finished, he lighted a cigarette and sent the car rushing through the darkness once more, a veritable meteor of speed.

He came into Exeter as the sky was greying in the east, and driving up the high street, turned into a side road. Here he stopped the car and got out. It had served its purpose and was now more of a liability than an asset. He left it standing by the side of the kerb and continued his journey on foot. The flat he was making for was situated in the better-class district — a new block that had been wet from the painters and decorators when he had taken it.

The building was not a large one, and there was no night porter, a fact which had recommended it to him. He opened the door of the main entrance with his key, and went up to the top floor in the automatic lift, sighing with relief when he closed his own front door behind him.

Switching on the lights, he made his way to the little kitchenette, where he knew there was a plentiful stock of tinned food and drink. Quickly and methodically he prepared himself a meal. It was a long time since he had eaten, and he was hungry. When he had finished eating, he turned his attention to the bag containing the diamonds.

With the aid of a chisel he found in a cupboard in the hall, he prised open the lock and feasted his eyes on the contents. Several times he allowed the smooth, grey-green pebbles to trickle through his fingers; and when he finally went into his bedroom, he took the bag for which he had risked his neck with him.

Undressing, he slipped into the comfortable bed, and composed himself for the rest his whole soul craved. His last waking thought before he fell asleep was admiration for his own cleverness, and the way he had succeeded in getting away with the diamonds in spite of all the difficulties he had had to overcome.

Could he have seen what was then transpiring at Stoneford, he would not have slept so peacefully; for he had made one mistake, and that mistake was to prove his undoing.

22

The Pursuit

'He may be anywhere,' said Trevor Lowe dubiously. 'The tracing of the car is practically impossible. We can neither give a description of it nor the man, for we don't know either. And if he's clever he won't stick to the car. He'll abandon it somewhere as soon as it has served his purpose.'

He was sitting with Shadgold and the chief constable in the charge-room of the little police station at Stoneford. All three were looking rather white and ill and drinking coffee, very black and very strong.

Major Strickland passed a trembling hand across his forehead; his head was aching abominably. 'What was that infernal stuff he used?' he asked.

'I don't know,' answered Lowe. 'Some highly concentrated gas, I should think. Probably in a liquid form and enclosed in a glass container, judging from the pieces of broken glass we found by the side of the bed.'

'I saw him throw the thing into the room,' said Shadgold, 'but after that I don't remember any more until I found Mr. White bending over me.'

'He was awake and listening for my signal,' said the dramatist. 'When nothing happened and he heard the fellow leaving, he guessed that something was wrong, and came into my bedroom. As soon as he saw that the three of us were unconscious, he blew the whistle as a signal to Rooper and his men.'

'And the damned fools let him get away,' grunted Shadgold. 'And it's a hundred chances to one if we ever get him again.'

Trevor Lowe nodded wearily. 'Yes, I feel rather guilty. After all, the whole scheme was mine, and it's failed.'

'I don't think there's any blame attaching to you, old chap,' muttered Strickland. 'It's devilish awkward, but it can't be helped.'

'I'm going to get hauled over the coals at the Yard,' said Shadgold morosely, 'unless we can get the man and the diamonds back soon. I was on the spot, and he got away right under my nose.'

Inspector Rooper, looking very tired and weary, came out of his little office and walked over to them. His wounded arm was suspended in a rough sling, and he was rubbing it ruefully.

'Painful?' asked Lowe.

The inspector made a grimace. 'It is rather, sir,' he replied. 'I've been trying to get 'old of Dr. Macaulay, but apparently he isn't at 'ome. Anyway, the man I sent down can't make anybody 'ear.'

'Must be out attending to a patient,' remarked Strickland.

'I expect that's it, sir,' said Rooper, 'It's a bit of a nuisance, because I want 'im to 'ave a look at poor Wilkins. He's dead, of course, and I've 'ad him removed to the mortuary, but I'd like to get Dr. Macaulay's report as soon as possible. 'Odges left a note asking 'im to come to the station as soon as 'e got back.'

'In the meantime,' grunted Shadgold, 'our man is gettin' further and further away, an' we're doin' nothing to stop him.' He rose and began to pace irritably up and down the dingy room.

'We can't do anything,' said Strickland. 'If we had a description of the man or the car, we could send out an all-station call and hope for the best. But without either, we're helpless.'

They lapsed into a gloomy silence. Lowe was feeling rather uncomfortable. Although they had all been very nice about it, he felt that he was entirely to blame. The whole scheme had been his, and it had been badly bungled. He should have taken more precautions. He sat staring into the red embers of the charge-room fire, and racked his brains to try and find some plan by which he could retrieve his position. Suddenly he looked up.

'Tell me,' he said, addressing Major Strickland, 'how long has Macaulay lived here? A year, isn't it?'

'About that. A little under, I think,' answered the chief constable, looking rather surprised. 'Why?'

'Just a minute; don't hurry me,' said Lowe. 'I'm trying to think something out. That means that Macaulay, Sedgwick and Jensen practically came to Stoneford together.'

'What are you getting at?' growled Shadgold, stopping abruptly in his pacing.

'I don't know,' answered the dramatist. 'I may not be getting at anything. Just let me go on. The man who got away with those diamonds tonight used a gas which it's doubtful he could've obtained anywhere around here unless he made it himself. The most likely person to know how to make that gas, and the person who could manufacture it most easily, would be a doctor.'

'Good God!' exclaimed Shadgold. 'Are you suggesting — '

'I'm not suggesting anything,' said Lowe. 'I'm just thinking aloud. Listen. Macaulay came to Stoneford at the same time as Jensen and Sedgwick. Macaulay would know the ingredients of that gas and how to make it. Macaulay is not at home. Now sort that out.'

'It's incredible,' protested Major Strickland, but Shadgold interrupted him.

'It may be incredible, sir,' he snapped, 'but it gives us a line to work on. And even if Mr. Lowe's wrong, it can't do any harm. I suggest we go down to Dr. Macaulay's place at once.'

There followed a slight argument. Major Strickland considered the whole idea absurd, and Rooper was inclined to agree with him. The Scotland Yard man, however, backed up by Lowe, overruled their objections. Hodges was sent to fetch the chief constable's car, and when it arrived they got in and drove down the little high street to the cottage that Dr. Macaulay occupied. The place was in darkness, and repeated knockings failed to elicit any response.

'He hasn't come home yet, anyway,' said Shadgold. 'What do we do now?'

'What I'd like to do,' said Lowe, 'is to have a look inside the house.'

'I'm afraid you can't do that, sir,' remarked Inspector Rooper. 'We've no authority to break in.'

'Listen to me,' said Lowe sharply. 'How long ago is it since you sent Hodges down to try and find Macaulay — about two hours, isn't it? Do you think it's likely he'd be with a patient all that time at this hour of the night?'

'I don't know that it's likely, sir,' said Rooper, 'but it's possible.'

'On the other hand,' said Lowe rapidly,

'supposing he's the man we're after — supposing he's gone and has no intention of coming back — every minute that passes is giving him a better opportunity to get clean away. I'm nothing to do with the law — I'm not bound by officialdom and red tape. Let me take the risk of breaking in.'

Shadgold looked dubious. 'Breaking into a private residence is a serious matter,' he began.

'So is murder,' snapped Lowe angrily. 'The man we're after has killed three people — remember that. Apart from which, he tried to kill me and very nearly succeeded, so I've got a personal grudge against him. What do you say? I'm warning you, he may never come back, and the more time we waste the less likely we are to ever catch him.'

It may have been that his argument prevailed, or it may have been — and this was more likely — that Inspector Shadgold had visions of facing an irate commissioner when he got back to London, and was willing to take any risk to avoid this unpleasant possibility. Whatever the reason was, he capitulated. 'If you've no objection, sir,' he said, looking at Strickland, 'I haven't, and there's something in what Mr. Lowe says.'

The chief constable shrugged his shoulders. 'It's unorthodox,' he said, 'but — carry on.'

Lowe waited for no more. Leaving the little group standing on the porch, he made his way round to the side of the cottage. The first two windows he tried were fastened, but at the back he found a small window that was partly open. Pulling himself up onto the sill, he wriggled his way through and found himself standing inside a tiny scullery. Everything was in complete darkness, but, striking a match, he was able by its feeble glimmer to make his way into the sitting room, and here he found an oil lamp, which he lighted. A second later he was out in the hall, and had opened the front door for the others.

'Here's the note Hodges left,' said the dramatist when they were inside, stooping and picking up a folded scrap of white paper. 'We'd better make a search of the house as quickly as we can.'

They started with the downstairs rooms, but found nothing until they reached the bedroom, and here there were obvious signs of a hasty departure. Drawers had been pulled open, and their contents lay scattered about the floor. The open wardrobe contained nothing but an old tweed suit; the rest of the clothing had gone.

'I think our burglary was justified,' said Lowe softly as he looked around him.

'I think so, too,' grunted Shadgold. 'Let's see if we can find anything that will give us a clue to where the fellow's gone. In the meantime — ' He turned to Rooper. ' — you go back to the station, Inspector, and send out a call with a description of Macaulay and the car.'

Rooper nodded and went off on his errand. After he had gone Strickland, the Scotland Yard man and Trevor Lowe began a methodical search of the cottage. They found nothing until they came to the tweed suit that was hanging in the wardrobe; and then Shadgold, who was searching the pockets, brought to light a crumpled scrap of paper. On it were a few lines of pencilled writing, and, reading it, he uttered an exclamation.

'I believe we've got something, sir,' he

said, his voice trembling with suppressed excitement.

Lowe looked over his shoulder. 'Dwight & Campbell,' he read, '26 High Street, Exeter. Who are they?'

'I can tell you that,' put in Major Strickland. 'They're a firm of estate agents.'

'Are they?' said the dramatist. 'Then I think they may be able to help us in locating Macaulay's present hiding-place.'

'We'll start right away for Exeter now,' said Shadgold, thrusting the paper into his pocket. 'I take it we can use your car, sir?'

'Of course,' said the chief constable. 'I'll drive you.'

Ten minutes later they were well on the way to Exeter.

23

The Kill

Their first stop was at the offices of Dwight & Campbell. By the time they reached Exeter, the sun was well up and the early-morning workers were starting off on their day's toil. But the firm of Dwight & Campbell had not yet begun business.

They had to hang about for nearly an hour and a half before the office was opened, and then nearly another hour before Mr. Campbell, who was the only surviving member of the firm, put in an appearance.

'Let me see, let me see … ' he said, rubbing his chin and frowning when they had stated their business. 'The description of the man you want seems familiar.' He thought hard and touched a bell on his desk. 'Yes, the only person remotely resembling him is a Colonel Wyatt, who rented a place through us about six months ago. I remember him because in lieu of the usual references he paid a year's rent in advance. Said he'd only just arrived from abroad and knew no one in England.'

A clerk came in answer to his summons.

'Which was the flat we rented to Colonel Wyatt?' Mr. Campbell inquired.

'I'll look it up, sir,' said the clerk, and withdrew. He was gone barely a minute. 'The top-floor flat at Regent House, Dane Street,' he said, laying a card before his employer.

'That's the place.' Mr. Campbell nodded. 'I remember now.'

Inspector Shadgold rose. 'Thank you, sir,' he said, 'I'm much obliged to you.'

He took his leave of the estate agent, and with the others left the office. They left the car at the end of Dane Street and approached Regent House on foot. The lift carried them to the top floor, and on the way up Lowe suggested a plan to which the others agreed.

There was no difficulty in finding the flat, for there was only one on this landing. Going up to the front door, Lowe gave a sharp knock, and at the same time uttered the call that has made the milkman such a heartily disliked member of the community. There was a pause, a shuffling step, and then the door was opened.

'Dr. Macaulay,' I think, said Trevor Lowe pleasantly.

The man's hand flew to his pocket and he whipped out his pistol. Shadgold, however, had been watching him; and before he could press the trigger the inspector launched himself forward, thirteen stone of flesh and bone.

The charge was a balanced one. It began at the right moment and ended at the right moment, and as it ended the Scotland Yard man's bunched right fist met Dr. Macaulay's jaw. The pistol exploded harmlessly with a deafening report, and the man went down, the automatic flying from his hand.

The bullet came so close to Lowe that it stirred the hair on his head. Then, with a howl of rage, Macaulay was up again. Shadgold's fist had landed an inch out for a knock-out.

With a horrible, snarling noise in his throat like a savage animal, Macaulay hurled himself at the detective, and Shadgold's knee came up with great force. The other gave a cry, half-groan, half-scream, and for the second time he fell. But this time he did not rise; he rolled this way and that upon the landing, his face contorted with pain.

'That's got him, I think,' snapped Shadgold, bending over the fallen man.

The pain died out of Macaulay, and he struggled to his knees, feeling dizzy and sick. A hand grasped his wrists and brought them together, then slipped on something cold and heavy that jangled horribly. The mist began to clear from his eyes and he tried to laugh. A sound came from his dry throat, but it was not the sound that he had intended. Looking up, he saw Inspector Shadgold and beside him Trevor Lowe and the chief constable. Shadgold was speaking.

' ... There'll be other charges. The murder of Elmer N. Jensen, the murder of Sedgwick alias Scanlon, the murder of Box.'

Macaulay came unsteadily to his feet, and a hand fell heavily on his shoulder. Vaguely he heard the inspector's words, but the only two that penetrated his dazed senses were his own name and murder.

His eyes, bloodshot and fearful, met those of Trevor Lowe. 'You devil!' He whispered the words almost under his breath, yet so clearly that every syllable was audible. 'You bloody clever devil! I suppose I've got to thank you for this, but you'll never hang me — '

'Look out!' shouted Lowe, bounding forward; for with his final word, Macaulay had straightened up. He seemed for an instant to tower over them like a giant. His hair was rumpled and his eyes flamed with a wild light. His shoulder caught Shadgold in the chest, and the Scotland Yard man fell sprawling on the tiled floor.

They saw what Macaulay was going to do. The landing window with a thirty-foot drop beyond was his objective, and he nearly reached it. But Lowe managed to grip the flying skirts of his dressing gown in time and pulled him back. Macaulay fought desperately, but by this time Shadgold had regained his feet, and he and Strickland went to Lowe's assistance.

Their captive was borne to the ground by sheer force of numbers; his last effort had been a failure.

* * *

Macaulay — or Menshaw, to give him his right name — faced the ordeal of his trial stoically, an impassive figure with an expressionless face that heard the death sentence without flinching. Every effort of the defence was swept aside, and although he steadily refused to make any statement, the evidence of his guilt was so great that the jury brought in a verdict of guilty without leaving the box.

A week before the date of the execution, however, Menshaw made a statement in which he confessed his guilt and cleared up several points that had remained obscure. It was found in this statement that O'Hara's story of the diamonds had been correct, and Menshaw had recovered consciousness from that attack on the lonely road outside Chicago with one idea in his mind — to get even with the men who had robbed him, and recover his property. It had taken him a long time to trace O'Hara and Scanlon, but eventually he had succeeded in connecting Elmer N. Jensen, the owner of Ridgeway Manor, with the man he was seeking.

Menshaw, who was a fully qualified doctor, and had once been in practice until some trouble over the death of one of his patients necessitated him giving it up, learned that the old village doctor had died and that his practice was vacant. He bought it and came down to Stoneford as Dr. Macaulay. He had grown a moustache and dyed his hair; and these changes in his appearance, together with a spurious Scottish accent, rendered his recognition by O'Hara impossible. As Dr. Macaulay, he was able to keep an eye upon his enemy and at the same time earn a fairly comfortable living — a necessity, since he was by no means well off.

O'Hara and Scanlon used to hold frequent meetings in a little wood just off Blackbarrow Coombe, and Menshaw had several times followed them and listened to their conversation. In this way he had discovered that O'Hara was still in possession of the diamonds and was trying to sell them to a man called Govin. Menshaw laid his plans to get possession of the stones and also his revenge on O'Hara, and a stroke of luck enabled him to use as an accomplice

Box, the landlord of the Black Moor Inn. He had recognized the fellow one day in the village as a man who had been mixed up with him in several shady schemes in America, and who had been responsible for the shooting of a patrolman during one of their exploits.

Menshaw decided that the inn on the moor would be the very place for his purpose. He wrote to O'Hara, making an appointment to meet him there, signing it Govin, and asking him to bring the diamonds with him. He registered and posted the letter in Princetown, and at the same time sent another to Box recalling the incident of the shot policeman in America and saying that he would call and see him on a matter that would be worth a hundred pounds to him. This letter he signed with his own name, Menshaw.

O'Hara, thinking the letter was from the real Govin, with whom he had been negotiating, kept the appointment, but he only took one of the stones as a sample. This upset Menshaw's plans, for he had anticipated the lot. He had already planned to kill O'Hara at the inn and place his body under the gravel to make it look like an accident, and in his rage he carried out this plan, suffocating O'Hara with a cushion so as to avoid any marks of violence.

It was only after the murder was committed that he realized that he had been premature, and that he should have first of all forced from O'Hara the whereabouts of the diamonds. He tried to rectify this error when he called on Scanlon — otherwise known as Sedgwick — but the man didn't know where the stones were hidden. He put up a fight, however, and Menshaw killed him, partly to keep his mouth shut and partly because it had always been his intention that both his adversaries pay in the same way for that double-cross on the lonely country road.

His efforts to obtain the whereabouts of the stones from Dorothy Jensen, and his attempt to put Lowe out of the running, were all set down in detail. On a cold morning a week after he had signed the statement, Menshaw walked firmly to the death-house and paid the penalty for his many crimes.

Dorothy Jensen and John Leyton were married in the early spring, taking up their permanent residence at Ridgeway Manor after a brief honeymoon abroad.

The final echo of the case reached Trevor Lowe just before the following Christmas, when Shadgold dropped in to inform the dramatist that the diamonds had been claimed by a syndicate that was now working the ravine where Menshaw had originally found the stones.

'So that's the last of that,' remarked the dramatist.

Shadgold helped himself to one of Lowe's cigars and bit off the end thoughtfully. 'There's only one thing that's never been cleared up,' he said, 'and that's the meaning of the words Rooper heard Sedgwick say to Jensen in the Coombe.'

Trevor Lowe shook his head. 'We shall never know that now,' he said, 'but I think Sedgwick had discovered that Jensen had been double-crossing him in some way over the diamonds. It would account for why Jensen went to meet Govin, as he thought, without saying anything to his accomplice.'

'You're probably right,' said the Scotland Yard man; and after he had finished his cigar and a drink, he took his departure.

'Well, White,' said Lowe with a twinkle in his eye, 'so much for fact. Now let's turn to fiction. If you'll bring me the draft of that second act, we'll get back to work!'

MURDER IN MANUSCRIPT
THE GLASS ARROW
THE THIRD KEY
THE ROYAL FLUSH MURDERS
THE SQUEALER
MR. WHIPPLE EXPLAINS
THE SEVEN CLUES
THE CHAINED MAN
THE HOUSE OF THE GOAT
THE FOOTBALL POOL MURDERS
THE HAND OF FEAR
SORCERER'S HOUSE
THE HANGMAN
THE CON MAN
MISTER BIG
THE JOCKEY
THE SILVER HORSESHOE
THE TUDOR GARDEN MYSTERY
THE SHOW MUST GO ON
SINISTER HOUSE
THE WITCHES' MOON
ALIAS THE GHOST
THE LADY OF DOOM
THE BLACK HUNCHBACK
PHANTOM HOLLOW
WHITE WIG

with Chris Verner:

THE BIG FELLOW

We do hope that you have enjoyed reading this large print book.

Did you know that all of our titles are available for purchase?

We publish a wide range of high quality large print books including:
Romances, Mysteries, Classics
General Fiction
Non Fiction and Westerns

Special interest titles available in large print are:
The Little Oxford Dictionary
Music Book, Song Book
Hymn Book, Service Book

Also available from us courtesy of Oxford University Press:
Young Readers' Dictionary
(large print edition)
Young Readers' Thesaurus
(large print edition)

For further information or a free brochure, please contact us at:
Ulverscroft Large Print Books Ltd.,
The Green, Bradgate Road, Anstey,
Leicester, LE7 7FU, England.
Tel: (00 44) 0116 236 4325
Fax: (00 44) 0116 234 0205

JESSICA'S DEATH

Tony Gleeson

Detectives Jilly Garvey and Dan Lee are no strangers to violent death. Nevertheless, the brutal killing of an affluent woman, whose body is found in a decaying urban neighborhood miles from her home, impacts them deeply. Their investigative abilities are stretched to the limit as clues don't add up and none of the possible suspects seem quite right. As they dig deeper into the background of the victim, a portrait emerges of a profoundly troubled woman. Will they find the answers they need to bring a vicious killer to justice?

WHITE WIG

Gerald Verner

A passenger is found shot dead in his seat on a London bus when it reaches its terminus. Apart from the driver and conductor, there have only been two other passengers on the bus, a white-haired man and a masculine-looking woman, who both alighted separately at earlier stops. To the investigating police, the conductor is the obvious suspect, and he is held and charged. The man's fiancée hires private detective Paul Rivington to prove his innocence — and it turns out to be his most extraordinary and dangerous case to date . . .

THE GHOST SQUAD

Gerald Verner

Mingling with the denizens of the underworld, taking their lives in their hands, and unknown even to their comrades at Scotland Yard, are the members of the Ghost Squad — an extra-legal organization answerable to one man only. The first Ghost operative detailed to discover the identity of the mastermind behind the buying and selling of official secrets is himself unmasked — and killed before he can report his findings to the squad. Detective-Inspector John Slade is his successor — but can he survive as he follows a tangled trail of treachery and murder?